# Rank Outsiders

by

CW00841583

Charlie De Luca

© Charlie De Luca, 2014

To my fabulous family.

Per ardua ad astra

Edited by My Cup Of Tea

www.charliedeluca.co.uk

# Rank Outsiders


## Chapter 1


Andrea Sheridan, Manager of the Looked After Children's Team, was frowning and hovering at the end of Poppy's desk. Poppy knew that look. It usually meant that she was going to get some extra work and that Andrea was thinking about how best to phrase her request. Poppy politely extricated herself from her telephone call and explained to the foster carer, Val Brown that she would talk to Neil about his behaviour, arranged to visit and replaced the receiver.

Andrea gave her an expectant look.

'Sorry to intrude, but I've just had Tina on the 'phone and she's likely to be off for at least a month.' Andrea dragged her fingers through her immaculate bob and pursed her lips. 'So, I'm having to reallocate Tina's work in the interim. Everyone has had three cases but in view of your heavy workload, I have decided to give you just the one.' Andrea waited, as though expecting a round of applause.

Poppy nodded. She often thought that the art of being a manager was to be able to hand out massive amounts of work, whilst at the same time convince your staff that you were really doing them a huge favour. Sort of work them into the ground but make them bloody grateful for the privilege. Andrea raised her eyebrows as though expecting a bit more enthusiasm. So, Poppy smiled and waited for the catch.

'I have allocated you Kyle Devlin. He's fab really, a total sweetie. I'm sure you will get along just fine.'

Poppy tried to remember what she knew about Kyle. Tina worked in the same office and often spoke about her cases, or she overheard snippets of information and conversations. Then it came to her.

'Isn't he the one that is with foster carers in Walton, who has just started work in the racing yard with the Trenthams? You know, the place where that other boy worked, the one who died?'

Andrea looked momentarily disconcerted and chewed her lip.

'Well, poor David Fenton was working at Trenthams when he was involved in the hit and run, it's true. Poor lad. They never did find out who mowed him down and left him for dead. Tina was rather upset.'

That was an understatement. Poppy remembered Tina and the staff from the Children's Home speaking in hushed tones, pale and shocked after the funeral. Tina had been hit especially hard. David Fenton had been something of a success story having overcome a terrible background to achieve some stability and success. By all accounts he had loved the horses and being small in stature had been hoping to become a jockey. It was a far cry from his abusive home where his father had bullied the life out of him, leaving him with bruises and fractures that would heal with time. The huge emotional scars and a pronounced stammer were much more difficult to deal with and would have persisted throughout his life, had he lived. She remembered Tina noting with pride, that he never stammered when he was dealing with the horses assigned to him and he was showing enthusiasm and passion for his job, as well as maintaining his employment. It may not seem much to other people, but for someone with his background it was a fantastic achievement. Everyone was delighted for him.

And then his life had been cut short in horrific circumstances. Dreadful, poor kid.

'The only thing is that as Kyle has recently started work, you will need to visit this afternoon and check out how it's going. I think the visit is overdue from what I remember. There's some other paperwork to complete but it should be an interesting visit and Mr Trentham, Jeremy, is so lovely.' Andrea patted her hair and fluttered her eyelashes. 'He gave me some brilliant tips when I went with Tina. I won £75 on one of them, a long shot it was, but Jeremy knew he was a safe bet. Do tell him that Andrea sends her regards, won't you?'

Poppy sighed, wondering if Jeremy knew that he was Andrea's latest crush. Happily married with grown up children, her boss certainly appreciated other men, but Poppy assumed it was in theory rather than actual practice. Oh well. She had been hoping to get away early as her temples were throbbing, and she needed to clear her head. But that wasn't going to happen now. She noticed that Andrea hadn't even asked her if she was free this afternoon. Probably, she had simply peeked in her diary, which was open on the desk, saw the empty space and made assumptions.

As if on cue, Andrea jabbed her manicured pink tipped forefinger at the blank lines in Poppy's diary.

'I couldn't help but notice you had space...'

Honestly, Poppy could swear that Andrea could read her mind sometimes. It was really quite uncanny. Still at least she could call in on her grandparents who lived in Walton and had done so for many years. With a career minded mother, jet setting all over the world for her jewellery business and a father who was remarried, sometimes Poppy thought they were more like parents to her than grandparents. She adored Millicent and George, as they insisted on being called. The thought of visiting them cheered her immensely. Then Poppy noticed Andrea's look of satisfaction at having managed to off load the visit on to her and felt mildly irritated.

'Thanks, Poppy. I'd go myself, but I've got back to back meetings.' Andrea explained. 'You'll love Kyle and all those gorgeous racehorses. It will all be perfectly straightforward.' Poppy should have known at the time that this was a sure sign that her visit to the Trenthams' Yard would be anything but.

Having managed to grab a paracetamol, washed down by a quick coffee, Poppy set out for Walton. Her headache started to clear. It was a bright November day, warm for autumn and she found that the drive to the yard was quite relaxing. As the scenery became progressively more rural, Poppy's thoughts turned to the young man she was about to meet, and she wondered how she should conduct the visit. She had quickly looked at his file and found that Tina hadn't seen Kyle for some weeks, so his visit was well overdue. Although, visits to children in care who are settled in placement are laid down in statute as being once every three months, the Yorkshire local authority for which she worked, had pledged to visit children at least every month to monitor progress and iron out any difficulties. So, she had better call in at the foster carers on the way back and see how things were going from their perspective. Kyle had been in placement with the foster carers, the Blooms, for just over a year and apart from some initial difficulties with school, behaviour and attitude, things seemed to be going relatively well and he was now in full time work. She learned that contact with Kyle's birth parents, a drug using mother and aggressive father, usually unsettled him. However, he hadn't seen his parents for some months, so had adjusted well to his placement.

Poppy had been a qualified social worker for three years and enjoyed her role. The heady idealism of her early days had been replaced with a much more realistic view of what could be achieved, and she had learned to celebrate small, positive changes in the young people she managed on her caseload. They were without exception funny and likeable, it was just that they were often so damaged by their early experiences that real progress was often very slow. But you just had to keep chipping away. All too often they were rank outsiders in terms of achievement and struggled to become productive adults. She felt it was her job to narrow those odds. She believed they could achieve great things. Her thoughts turned to David Fenton and the tough circumstances that other youngsters are born into. Some of the kids' stories took her breath away. Starting out, Poppy realised she had been rather naïve and had taken her stable, loving but messy family very much for granted. Therefore, the acts of extreme cruelty and depravity that many of the children had had to cope with, never ceased to shock and upset her. Now, she knew that life was far from fair and that she had been dealt a much better set of cards than many. She saw it as her responsibility, therefore, to advocate for those young people on her caseload, defend their rights and nurture them when the need arose. She also needed to point out to them when their choices and behaviour were leading them into difficulties. It was a challenging but nonetheless rewarding role. Poppy loved it as each day was different and totally unpredictable. Like today, for example.

It was Friday and with the weekend looming, inevitably she thought about Jamie. The issue of Jamie was a thorny one that she was struggling to deal with. They had been together for two years when he suddenly announced he needed space and that things were moving too fast for him. Poppy had been very confused. A two year relationship with no suggestion of moving in together or heaven forbid, marriage, could hardly be described as fast, in Poppy's view. She immediately thought that his explanation was a euphemism for 'I've fallen out of love with you' or 'I've met someone else.' She had been devastated but knew with time that she'd get over it.

Poppy had been honest enough to admit that the first flush of romance had worn off, then she and Jamie had settled into a relationship borne of habit and possibly fear of the unknown. Neither had wanted to end things. Then, Jamie had finished it and after a month or so of soul searching she was starting to feel much better, even a bit liberated as she began to mull over the possibilities that life may offer her. But, Jamie hadn't quite gone away. It was as if he couldn't bring himself to finally sever all ties. He still telephoned her, they went on occasional nights out and crucially he still expected to stay the night. Initially, she had been pleased about this, seeing it as a sign of reconciliation, but now she was starting to feel used and irritated by him. It was very much a case of Jamie wanting his cake and eating it and she was becoming heartily sick of him having everything his own way. He had the advantage of appearing to be single and yet the benefit of regular sex if he wanted it. Poppy was faintly disgusted with herself for capitulating time after time. Yet, she too, found it difficult to break away. He would click his fingers and she would go running. She realised she had to stop things now. She was starting to hate herself for being so weak. This weekend, she told herself, she would simply not be available when he called. Bugger him. She would just go out with her housemates, Hannah and Maisy, instead.

The fields stretched out ahead of her, interspersed with trees and bright sunshine. The Yorkshire landscape was picturesque, even in November. As she approached the village of Walton, she wondered about the place she was visiting. She wasn't sure what to expect. She knew very little about horses and was even a little bit scared of them to be perfectly honest. She didn't share her grandparents' love of betting or having a 'flutter' as they described it. Still, it was Kyle she had come to see, and she presumed the horses would all be safely stabled away. She might be able to get away with giving them a cursory glance, mutter a few platitudes and leave it at that. The road narrowed, and she passed a sign telling her to '*Slow Down -Horses in Training*'. This confirmed that she must be on the right track. From the corner of her eye, she could see a dark horse cantering around in the field besides the road just ahead of her. His gorgeous dark conker colour was set off by the red rug he wore. For a second, she was utterly transfixed by its sheer beauty as the animal snorted, slowed and trotted up to the paddock fencing, its tail held high. Abruptly, the creature turned back and then galloped full pelt towards the fence. She expected it to slide to a dramatic halt before the rails. Instead, it continued and soared over the fence in a perfect arc, galloping right over the road ahead of her. She screamed and jammed her feet onto the brakes. She tried to swerve and waited for the seemingly inevitable crunch of horse upon steel, as her heart pounded painfully in her chest.

# Chapter 2

Tristan Davies was a very lean, fair haired man who wore the casual uniform of a man in his profession. This was a padded green jacket, cream jodhpurs and short jodhpur boots. He listened intently as Jeremy Trentham, a dark handsome fellow who was slightly running to fat, went through the entries for the next few weeks. The National Hunt season had just begun and the guvnor had lots of plans and ideas. More importantly Jeremy's star was rising, and he had some really promising horses this season. Having been out with the string that morning and schooled later, Tristan was feeling excited, like a kid before Christmas, about the forthcoming season. This was his second year with the Trenthams as their stable jockey and he had been an apprentice with them before that. Life was good. He was injury free which was a blessing for a jump jockey and Jeremy had installed him in a nearby cottage away from the lads' quarters. He was paid a decent retainer and was still free to take other rides provided they didn't clash with their runners. Next week he was riding the excellent Benefactor, aka Bennie, in a decent hurdle race at Haydock. From the feel of him this morning, it was not only Tristan who was relishing the season ahead.

'How did you think Bennie went in training?' Jeremy asked.

Tristan nodded. 'Great. He felt really well. I'm sure we'll be in with a shout if he can go the distance.'

Jeremy nodded, clearly pleased. 'Yep. Well, let's hope so.'

Laura, Jeremy's wife wandered in with a couple of steaming mugs of tea. She wore her dark hair to her shoulders and had the slightly weather beaten complexion of a woman used to the great outdoors. Even in her casual clothes, she had the look of the country set about her and wore a big furry headband and brown, leather Dubarry boots along with her own expensive brand of quilted jacket.

'Here, Nelson.' She threw a treat to the spaniel, who leapt out of his bed to retrieve it and bounced around hoping for more. Then he pricked up his ears and ran to the door barking excitedly.

'Hush now,' muttered Jeremy. 'It's probably just Barry,' he shouted to his wife as she went to answer the door, referring to their head lad.

The two men continued their discussions until Laura came back with a small, pale girl, clutching an enormous diary to her. She was trembling so much that her voice came out all high and quivery as tears streaked her cheeks.

' Erm, I've come to see Kyle, but I think I've hit one of your horses as I drove in...'


Following the safe return of the redoubtable Benefactor back to his stable, there was the inevitable post mortem about how the horse had escaped. Jeremy, Laura, Tristan, Poppy and a man who introduced himself as Basil, were all sitting round the kitchen table.

'Well, Bennie seems fine after his little adventure. I've got Mickey hosing his legs just in case. But how on earth did he get out, that's the question? Someone must have forgotten to close the bolt correctly. Who's his lad again?' Jeremy ran his fingers through his greying temples. It was clear from his voice that he was struggling to keep his equilibrium and the fact that he had guests was probably the only reason he hadn't blown his top. He noticed his wife giving him warning glances. Tristan missed them, however and blundered on.

'It's the new lad, Kyle, isn't it?'

Poppy jerked her eyes up at the mention of his name. Basil weighed up the situation. A suave man, with the looks of an ageing matinee idol, he neatly steered the conversation into safer waters. Poppy gathered that he was an owner and friend who had just happened to be at the yard at the time. It was Tristan, though, who had gone haring out at the speed of light to catch the stray animal, who was munching grass at the other side of the road when Tristan had caught up with him.

'Well, it could have been anyone, really. But all that matters, is that neither man nor beast were hurt and that is the main thing. I shudder to think what might have happened to this lovely lady if Bennie had hit her car.'

Poppy gave him a grateful look, ignoring the feminist in her that bristled at being described as a lady, as she nursed her strong mug of sweet tea. Thankfully her colour was returning, and she was starting to feel a little more human.

'Quite,' said Laura scowling at her husband. 'It must have been dreadfully frightening, a horse leaping out in front of you.'

Poppy managed a smile. 'It was something of a shock. I managed to swerve but I honestly thought I was going to hit it, Bennie, I mean.'

Laura gave her a considering look. 'Are you quite sure you don't want something a bit stronger, a shot of Scotch for example?'

Poppy shook her head. 'No, thanks. I'm feeling much better actually. Perhaps, I could see Kyle now?'

'Yes, of course. He'll be back now it's feed time.'

Poppy opened her diary. 'Great. There's a form for you to sign, by the way.' She passed it to Jeremy. 'How is Kyle doing overall, would you say?'

Jeremy thought for a moment. 'Oh, fine. He's quite a good worker actually and his riding is improving no end, isn't it? He has good hands...' Jeremy gave Poppy a slight smile. Poppy wrote this into her diary wondering what on earth 'good hands' meant. She was feeling too ill at ease to ask.

'So, what's happened to Tina did you say?' Laura was rather concerned about the impact this pretty, young social worker might have on the lads in the yard who barely gave homely looking Tina a second glance. Now this younger, slim version with her delicate face and huge eyes, was altogether a different matter.

'She will be off for a least a month, I believe, so I will work with Kyle during that period.'

'Right,' Laura gave a weak smile. 'Well, if you could just show Poppy where to find Kyle, would you Jeremy?'

However, Tristan was already on his feet and before she could object he managed to cut in.

'It's alright, Laura. I'll see to Poppy.' He studiously ignored her raised eyebrows.


They found Kyle in the barn filling hay nets.

'Here he is. Kyle, there's someone to see you.'

Poppy extended her hand. 'Hi there, Kyle. I'm Poppy Ford. I'm covering for your social worker, Tina Barratt, whilst she's off sick.' She took in the boys open face, his freckled nose, blue eyes and soft brown curls. 'Listen, is there anywhere we can talk? I just need to see how you're getting on and make sure you're OK.'

Kyle nodded. 'Yeah, is it alright if we use the grooms' room, Tris?'

'No problem, though I'm sure the guvnor would be happy to let you speak to Poppy inside the house.'

'No, I'm sure it will be fine,' replied Poppy firmly. She wanted to speak to Kyle on his own and wasn't sure she would be able to do that in the main house. Besides, she felt quite intimidated by the Trenthams and their cut glass accents and aura of confidence. Tristan nodded and withdrew.

Kyle led her off to a small room through where the tack, row upon row of saddles, bridles and all manner of horse wear, was kept. There was an overwhelming smell of leather and saddle soap which was not unpleasant. The room had a small gas heater, a table, chairs, a kettle and several mugs. There was also a much used dartboard, a Pirelli calendar featuring a naked, busty girl and piles of old papers stacked on the table. The papers were mainly copies of the Racing Post and were yellowed with age and much thumbed.

Kyle looked apologetically at the nude calendar. Poppy noticed this and appreciated his sensitivity. He was a lean youth, with wide open face. He wore a green quilted jacket and his curly hair had bits of hay sticking out of it. He gave her an appraising look and asked after Tina.

'She'll be off for a while. So, I'm sorry to just turn up and surprise you but your statutory visit is out of date and then there's your personal education plan that Tina started and I need to finish. Let's see...' Poppy fished in her bag for her diary. 'You've been here how long?'

'About a month or so. Yeah, it's fine. Hard work mind, but great.'

Poppy nodded, taking in his honest face. 'How do you get on with the other staff?'

Kyle frowned. 'You mean the lads? Alright, I think. Some live in but I come in everyday from Betty's. But it's fine, no problem...'

Poppy wrote everything down in her diary.

'Well, Mr Trentham seems pleased. He says you work hard and have good hands, whatever that means...'

Kyle grinned, clearly pleased. 'Did he? Great. That means I don't jab the horses in the mouth with their bit, just try and gently squeeze the reins to slow them down. Like brakes, see?' Kyle squeezed his hands onto imaginary reins, as if to illustrate this. 'Bits can be very harsh on the horses' mouths, you see.'

Poppy didn't see but let this pass. She realised she knew almost next to nothing about horses.

'Which horses do you look after?'

Kyle face split into a huge grin. 'Oh, I've got four sometimes five. There's Bennie, Paddy, Socks and Norman. Of course, they're just their stable names.'

Poppy frowned at the mention of Bennie. 'Oh, yes Bennie. He's the one I had a close encounter with just now. He leapt out in front of me onto the road. He seems to have got out of his stable somehow.'

Kyle scowled. 'Yeah, I heard about that. **They** think or rather Mickey thinks I didn't close the door properly but it's crap. I always do the bolt and the kick latch on the bottom of the door. Must have been someone else who went in and forgot, unless Bennie fiddled with the bolt himself.' Kyle frowned some more. 'Don't think I've seen him do it before, though.'

'Well, he's fine apparently, so no harm done.'

Kyle nodded, deep in thought. 'Well, I hope so. He's running in a few days. And he's me favourite. I'd be gutted in anything happened to him. He's a right softie.' He looked momentarily embarrassed to have revealed so much about his affection for the horse, but Poppy warmed to him all the more. 'Come on, I'll show you round.'

His enthusiasm was infectious. Poppy was treated to a tour of Kyle's horses and was amazed at the knowledge he had about them as he showed her each one in turn. Bennie was back in his stable, with a small, wiry man who she took to be Mickey, running his hands up and down his legs.

'He seems to be alright, lucky for you. Next time don't be so bloody careless, you bloody idiot,' he barked. When Poppy came into view, he wasn't at all embarrassed, but simply scowled further and continued massaging the horse's legs. Bennie was huge and dark brown or bay, as Kyle described him. He had a velvety muzzle and blew warm breath all over them as he hunted in Kyle's pockets for polos. Poppy was amazed. Then Kyle showed her Paddy, Norman and Socks. Socks was so named on account of the fact that he had four perfect white markings like ankle socks on each leg. Each stable was knee deep in straw and even to Poppy's untutored eye, the animals all looked relaxed, happy and in the pink. Kyle knew to pull Socks' ears, he liked that apparently, and stroke Norman between the eyes so that he virtually nodded off. Paddy was a huge grey horse with black kohl like rimmed eyes. He had a penchant for playing with zips. Poppy stayed well away from him, though the zipper of Kyle's jacket kept him entertained for a few minutes as he caught the tag and tried to pull it down.

After half an hour or so, Poppy felt she had enough information and was satisfied that Kyle was doing just fine. He wasn't in formal education, but his job provided training, as well as reasonable pay for a boy of sixteen. He was learning important skills such as the importance of reliability and improving his employment prospects, as well. But more than that, he was thriving. She popped in to see the Trenthams before she left. They seemed calmer now that Bennie was safe and assured her they would keep an eye on Kyle and prioritise his welfare.

'I'm just going to catch Mrs Bloom and have a chat with her. And I'll pop back in a couple of weeks. In the meantime, please ring me if there are any problems,' Poppy explained, having given them her work mobile number.

'No problems. I'll see you out then.' Kyle looked up from his mucking out and gave her a cheery wave. As she made her way to her car, Tristan ambled over.

'I'm sorry about your introduction to us, what with Bennie jumping out, the guvnor being touchy and Mickey being his usual pain in the arse. We are actually quite civilised when you get to know us, honestly. I'll be in The Yew tree later if you will let me buy you a drink, you know, to make up for things.'

Poppy was taken aback. She realised that the excessive gallantry was his way of hitting on her, but what the hell. She took in his blond good looks and crinkly blue eyes. She had thought jockeys were very short, but he was tall and slim, with endless legs. In her bag she heard the vibration of her mobile humming

16

away. It had been beeping on an off all afternoon. She knew without looking that it would be Jamie who was no doubt at a loose end and would be trying to make arrangements to meet up. She desperately wanted to avoid falling into that trap. It was time to move on. She had been looking for an excuse and here it had arrived, fallen into her lap, gift wrapped, albeit in a surprising form. She looked at Tristan uncertainly for a minute and decided she liked what she saw. She found herself hesitating, but only for a second.

'Thank you. I'd like that. I'm just going to call in on the Blooms first.' Tristan's grin nearly split his face in two. Poppy was charmed by his lack of guile.

'Brilliant. I'll be there from about seven.'

Poppy nodded. 'Ok, I'll catch you later then.'

The Blooms were a lovely couple, Poppy decided. They lived in a stone cottage at the edge of Walton with a vast, well tended garden. It reminded Poppy of the World War Two posters of 'dig for victory' with its rows of runner beans and sprouts. Even in the fading light, she could make out neatly trimmed hedges, a large greenhouse and perfect borders. The couple seemed a little old fashioned but were warm and kindly. Mrs Bloom was almost as broad as she was tall, with her hair twisted up into a bun. She insisted on making Poppy a cup of tea and giving her a slice of cake. Poppy felt like she could fall asleep, sitting in their deep chintz sofa next to the wood stove burner. She suddenly felt very tired, as she asked how Kyle was doing.

'He's a good lad, Kyle. He's been with us about a year. He struggled a bit at first and he missed his old carers who had to give up due to health problems. He was having contact with his mother at the time, but he's been much better since that was knocked on the head. A sight better. She promised him the earth and didn't deliver. It's often the way with these kids. The parents want shooting, if you ask me.'

Poppy smiled politely and noticed the photos of ex foster kids on the walls. Mrs Bloom followed her gaze.

'Twenty or so kids we've had, and they all come back to see us. Once a Bloom, always in Bloom, is our motto. Some of them have done very well. Have you heard of Tyler Dalton, midfielder for Manchester City? He was one of ours. Comes back regular though to see us. It's fantastic when they do well, it really is.' Mrs Bloom shifted her considerable girth and jabbed her finger at a photo of a whimsical looking, mixed race boy aged about seven. It was unmistakably Tyler. He was gappy toothed and fresh faced, but the familiar eyes stared back at her.

Mr Bloom wandered in from the garden with a basket full of potatoes and carrots.

'Are you telling her about Tyler? Spent hours I did running him all over as a youngster when he was signed to Hull City. Then he was spotted by Manchester City and the rest as they say is history. Mind, he did batter me plants, like, with all that kicking a ball about.' Poppy could imagine that Mr Bloom would have found this very difficult to cope with, but still, Tyler Dalton! Even Poppy had heard of him. He was the latest hot shot who was riding a crest of a wave from his stunning performances in recent weeks. There was even talk of a place on the England squad.

'Lass, do you want to take some back with you? We've plenty.' Mr Bloom inclined his head towards his basket of vegetables. 'You look like you need building up, you're all skin and bone. These will put you right, straight from the garden, they are. Kyle helps me with the gardening, too. He's getting the hang of it now.'

Poppy thanked him, but politely declined. Presumably, he was comparing her to his well upholstered wife. She tried to concentrate on the task in hand.

'So, do you have any worries about Kyle? He seems to be doing well at the yard. I've just come from there.'

Mrs Bloom shook her head. 'No lass. He gets a bit of joshing from the other lads and lassies. But it's only to be expected, that, with him being new, I reckon. What do you think, Bert?'

'Give over worrying about him. It's nothing he can't handle. The Trenthams are good sorts though and the head lad, Barry, will make sure it doesn't get out of hand. I see Barry in the pub now and again, so he keeps an eye on the lad. He'd let me know if anything was amiss.'

Poppy couldn't recall meeting Barry but was glad that Kyle had someone nearer his own age in a senior position who he could relate to and said as much.

'Oh, Barry's in his forties,' replied Mr Bloom, incredulous. 'They just call him a lad, because that what they always call grooms in racing yards, whatever their age, I suppose.'

Poppy tried to hide her blushes. The world of horse racing certainly had some unusual terminology, but she'd just have to try and learn about it for a month or so, at least whilst Tina was off. She had already learned about what having 'good hands' meant, as well as understanding about 'bits' and that dark brown horses were referred to as 'bay'.

'What are the long term plans for Kyle, do you know?'

'Well, we might be asked to foster him after he's eighteen since the law changed and he can stay with us. But if he wants to be an apprentice jockey and do that training at the College of Racing then I reckon he'd have to move out. But we'd be happy to keep him, if he wants to stay.' Poppy was pleased as things seemed to be working well and the Blooms were clearly very committed to Kyle staying with them.


She said her goodbyes, gave them her work mobile number and drove to her grandparents. They lived at the other end of the town in a stone farmhouse. They had moved to Walton when her grandfather retired from his job as a banker. They had moved from the city and had embraced the rural community. When she arrived, her grandmother, Millicent, hugged her warmly.

'What a lovely surprise, Poppy. How are you?'

George came in from walking the dog, a spaniel called Bertie. They were thrilled to find that Poppy had been to the racing yard.

'Splendid,' continued Millicent. 'I've just been watching the racing on the TV. I usually have a little flutter on the Trenthams' horses. We see them going to the gallops or doing road work all the time in the village. It's so exciting and

20

that stable jockey, Tristan Davies, is lovely. Perhaps, we'll see more of you now you have a client there. Maybe you could get us some red-hot tips?'

George gave her a baleful look. 'Now, now, Millicent. Don't get carried away.' George looked at Poppy. 'Milly had a treble come in the other day and won rather a lot of money. Don't let it go to your head, though.'

Her grandmother was unrepentant. 'Got to have a little pleasure in life. Anyway, it keeps my brain ticking over, just like these cryptic crosswords.' Millicent was a very spritely seventy year old and had a horror of going senile, so spent hours working out racing odds, Sudoku and crosswords to counter this. 'Now what will you have to eat, dear?'

Poppy was persuaded into eating a sandwich and a slice of one of her grandmother's courgette cakes. It sounded revolting but was absolutely delicious.

'Splendid cook, your grandmother.' George remarked, oozing with pride. 'How's your young man?'

Poppy nodded and said he was fine, rather than tell them the truth. She didn't want to tell anyone about their relationship breakdown until she had everything straight in her head. She was very undecided about Jamie. She realised she'd had about four more missed calls from him, complete with increasingly petulant text messages. With a sigh she had deleted them all. That would show him. Having spent a pleasant hour or so chatting, just after seven, she drove to The Yew Tree, subtly applied her lipstick, brushed her hair and made her way to the pub's lounge.


The Yew Tree was an old public house with beams, horse brasses and a roaring fire. Tristan bought her a white wine and settled down opposite her. She noticed he had changed his shirt and his hair was a darker blond, still damp from the shower. He gave her a wide smile.

'I wasn't sure you'd turn up, but I'm glad you did. So, have you recovered from your near miss with Bennie, then? You did look extremely pale.'

'Yes. It was just a shock. I was sure I was going to hit him. Thank God, I didn't. It could have been a very different story.' She smiled shyly.

'Well, Mickey has checked him over and put some herbal ointment on his legs, but we'll know more tomorrow if he's sound or not. I think he'll be fine. It's a bit of a mystery how he got out, though. We are all so careful, usually. Probably just one of those things.'

'I did ask Kyle, but he seemed genuinely perplexed. I met Mickey, though. He seemed very annoyed about it.'

Tristan grinned showing off white, even teeth. 'That's just his way. His lotions and potions and the stuff he cooks up using herbs and bits of roots are amazing, though. That's why the guvnor puts up with him, really. He uses old fashioned remedies, like comfrey for injuries, nettles for iron deficiency and clivers for inflammation. No antibiotics or modern medicine for him, but it works and it's all natural.'

Tristan kept looking at her glass and she had the distinct impression that he would leap up and buy her another drink in order to stop her leaving. The thought flattered and amused her.

'So, how often do you have to see Kyle, then?' Tristan's gaze was intent.

'Well, at least monthly, probably more if there's difficulties. And, of course, it all depends on how long Tina is off, I suppose.'

Tristan gave her an appraising look. 'Well, let's hope she takes her time coming back then.'

Poppy laughed. Although, she didn't anticipate seeing him again, it was certainly nice being chatted up. Tristan was straightforward and direct. It certainly made a pleasant change from trying to second guess what was going on in Jamie's head.

Poppy sifted through her emails after the weekend. There were rather a lot from The Emergency Duty Team regarding one of the girls on her caseload. Sadie Jones, aged twelve, had gone missing from 'The Limes' Children's Home after an argument. The staff had alerted the police who had visited and made inquiries with known associates to no avail. Then on Sunday she had turned up very much worse for wear, with a new mobile phone and her neck covered up her with a scarf, striding in as though nothing had happened. She had gone missing at the same time as another girl, Louella Simpson, fifteen, who seemed to have acquired some new clothes and a cocky attitude to match. However, the girls insisted they hadn't been together. Given the girls' vulnerability, there was a great deal of speculation about where they had been and how they had acquired their new items. Poppy sighed as she reached for the telephone. Either they had stolen clothes and 'phones or they had been given them by a person or persons unknown. Poppy was immediately suspicious. If they were given various expensive items, it had to be in return for doing God knows what. Either explanation was very worrying. Poppy arranged to visit that afternoon to try and find out what was going on.

She then went through the duty calls. She was on the rota for the morning and basically had to take calls for the whole team, attempting to deal with emergencies from foster carers, young people and their parents and queries from social workers in other teams. She worked her way through the messages which were of the usual type; a handful of missing kids, unhappy foster carers feeling at the end of their tether and requiring support, contact difficulties between kids in care and their parents and queries about finances or social work visits. There were also some queries from IRO's, Independent Reviewing Officers, who chaired the children's reviewed and made sure that the recommendations were carried out. Then she found a message for Tina from David Fenton's sister asking for a call back. This was the boy that had been killed in the hit and run who had worked previously at the Trenthams. Curiosity got the better of her and she decided to ring back, particularly as Tina was likely to be off for a while.

David's sister Tara, who was technically his half-sister, had gone into foster care rather than a residential children's home. But that placement had broken down and Poppy wasn't too sure what had happened to her afterwards. Perhaps, she was telephoning for an update on David's case? Poppy didn't even know if the hit and run was still open from a criminal point of view, but she could pass on her details to the police.

'I'm covering duty, so I thought I'd give you a ring back. I know you left a message for Tina, but she is off at the moment. What can I do to help?'

'Oh God. Does that mean she's not passed on what I told her last time?'

Poppy was confused. 'Sorry, I'm not sure. Do you want to tell me and then I can make sure and check the records? Did you want me to pass on a message?'

Tara paused. 'Well, it's difficult. It's about Davy. I'm wondering if he couldn't keep his mouth shut and that's what killed 'im. You know...' The words came out slurred. There was a long pause. Poppy couldn't tell if Tara had fallen asleep or had been cut off. She was definitely on something, but was it drugs or alcohol or both? She couldn't tell.

Poppy remembered her training on dealing with clients with addictions and spoke clearly and calmly. 'I'm afraid I don't know if Tina passed on the information or not. But if you tell me what the message was then, of course, I will make sure it gets passed on to the right department. We are all desperately sorry about David and the hit and run. If you have any information that might help the police catch the killers, then I really think you should contact them.'

Tara sighed, a world weary sound that was tinged with grief.

'Davy knew 'cos I told him, then he reckoned they were doing the same to them girls. You know, inviting them to parties and stuff. I told 'im don't do nothing, 'cos they'll get you. He said he couldn't stand by and do nothing, though. Now, I'm worried he told 'em what he thought and that's what got him killed...'

Poppy's mind was in a whirl. What on earth did she mean? Surely this had all been investigated by the police previously? She took a deep breath.

'Can I ask you to go into a bit more detail? What did you mean about the parties, what sort of parties? Are you suggesting anything untoward?'

There was a long, scornful silence. 'Yeah, of course. I reckon Davy tried to stop it, had a word with 'em. And now he's dead, 'cos he knew what was going on...'

The blood stilled in Poppy's veins.

'Have you told the police about this? I can transfer you if you just hang on. Listen, are you in any sort of trouble?'

'No, no police.' There appeared to be some sort of scuffle in the background. Poppy thought she heard another voice in the background. 'Got to go. Just tell that Andrea to ring me back. D'ya hear?'

Poppy fumbled about for a pen and notepad. It was important to take the phone number down accurately so that Andrea could return the call.

'Yes, of course, can I take your number?' She heard a click and then the line went dead.

Chapter 4

The Limes sounded rather grand but was far from it in reality. Situated in a council estate on the outskirts of York, it was in fact four council houses knocked into one. They were of the post war variety and created a rather solid, functional building. The large gardens of the four houses had all been pooled to provide a very large space and some staff members had had the idea of providing a poly tunnel to encourage the kids to get involved with planting and growing. It was innovative, but few of the kids had taken to it and now it was largely abandoned, like a huge plastic snake taking up a large part of the garden. The inside of the property had had no expense spared, but there had been frequent changes of sofas and soft furnishings due to the kids damaging things. The walls and general paintwork had had to be frequently updated for similar reasons. After all, how could kids with no respect for themselves be expected to take pride in their surroundings? For this was the place that kids with the most severe emotional difficulties ended up. Those too defiant, downright destructive and damaged for foster carers to cope with. Those whose early years had been characterised by instability, loss, neglect and abject cruelty. These young people were damaged and corrupted by those that were supposed to care for them, sometimes irretrievably. These were the young people who desperately needed the help and support that the staff were trained to give, but who were so often so full of mistrust and self-loathing that they were often unwilling or unable to accept it. They were not easy to help, far from it.

Staff did not have the right to lock the kids in and with physical restraint being increasingly frowned upon, it was sometimes difficult to know who was in charge; the kids or the staff. It was a short-term unit where kids were assessed, and routines and boundaries were slowly and painstakingly reinstated. School and education were reintroduced into the lives of those who had never valued it. Young people who responded well were moved swiftly on to more long term homes, making way for the more kids; unruly runaways, teenagers who had been abandoned or rejected or children whose foster placements had broken down. Staff had to again begin the painstaking process of introducing consistency, boundaries and support, all over again. Poppy felt that all of the staff were caring, concerned and very keen to make a difference, but it was not an easy job and certainly not one for the faint hearted.

She had written up Tara's message in as much detail as she could, sent an email to Andrea and put Tara's ramblings down to alcohol or drugs' consumption and quite possibly guilt. Surely the police had looked into David's death and spoken to Tara at length? Why did she want to drag everything up again? David had been one of those who had managed to turn his life around. He loved the job at the Trenthams and was due to move into supported lodgings nearer Walton. Then he was mowed down in a hit and run. His death was made all the more poignant by the fact that at long last he was shaking off his unpromising start in life.

Moira was a Senior Care Officer at The Limes and had endless resources of patience. A homely woman in her forties, she managed to combine humour and discipline at the same time which was no mean feat. She could calm a situation effortlessly by disarming a truculent youngster with humour, offer a range of choices objectively and without prejudice so eventually the young person would make the right choice and feel that it was their own decision whilst all the time Moira had been gently nudging them in that direction. The manager was the charismatic Lawrence Morgan whose commitment and passion for the young people in his care was unswerving and relentless. Today, The Limes was quiet with most of the kids being in schools or some other form of education albeit pupil referral units or behavioural units. On duty was Moira and another staff member, a lanky man with long hair called Nathan, who was helping the cook prepare an evening meal. Lawrence was ensconced in the office completing data returns. Poppy discovered that Sadie Jones, aged twelve, had been to school that morning having been persuaded eventually to attend by Moira's persistent manner.

'Sadie was rather tired this morning, so I had to really cajole her to get up and she's not in the best of moods. But I've not heard anything from school, so I presume she's OK and hasn't kicked off or walked out. So that's something, I suppose.'

'So, what is she saying about where she's been all weekend? Any clues? Have any of the other kids let anything slip?'

Moira shook her head. 'Nope, absolutely nothing, though you do know that Louella went missing about the same time, though they are not especially close so it's unlikely, but not impossible they went together. They are not admitting to it anyway. Somehow, I doubt they're in it together. But you never know.'

'Hmm. Anything else?'

'Well, she came back with a new mobile and a scarf tightly wrapped round her neck as I told you on the telephone, so I'm convinced she is trying to hide love bites or something, possibly a tattoo? And she was as pleased as punch with the new mobile.'

Poppy took this in. 'What sort of 'phone is it?'

'Well, I'd say a smart 'phone but probably one of the cheaper ones, but expensive enough for a freebie. She's either nicked it or been given it. Either way it's worrying. Someone wouldn't just give her a 'phone, would they? So, the question is if it isn't stolen, what has she done to acquire one? As we all know, there is no such thing as a free lunch.'

Poppy sighed. She was not looking forward to her audience with Sadie, who could be deliberately obtuse and downright rude when challenged. She would probably storm out again if she tackled her head on, so she decided to try a more circumspect route.

'Of course, if she was given a 'phone by this unknown person then now they have the perfect means of keeping in contact with her which may increase her absconding,' continued Moira thoughtfully.

'Do you think we would be justified in confiscating it? Shall we ask Lawrence?'

Lawrence heard his name being mentioned and wandered into the sitting room. In his thirties with his dark wavy hair worn to his collar, he was dressed stylishly in smart trousers and a maroon and pink striped shirt. He was, Poppy supposed, rather attractive, the sort of man her mother would describe as 'dishy'. Maybe he tried a bit too hard to look good, Poppy thought. Nonetheless, the kids seemed to like him and always sought him out if they felt hard done by or had a dispute with staff or other residents.

'Hi there, Poppy. What was it you wanted to ask me?'

'Hi. We were just wondering if we could justify confiscating Sadie's 'phone if she can't provide us with a reasonable explanation for how she came by it. What do you think?'

Lawrence mulled this over. 'Well, we can ask her to hand it over, but don't you think that might be a bit confrontational and give her the perfect excuse to run off again?' Lawrence's eyes widened as he had an idea. 'Whereas, if we simply ask her and appear to accept her explanation that way, she won't have an excuse to run away again. It's a 'pay as you go' I think, anyway, so the rate she's using it she will run out of credit very soon. Then we can refuse to top it up unless she gives us a plausible explanation for how she came by it. What do you think?'

Poppy beamed. Why didn't she think of that?

'That is pure genius. It's no wonder you are a manager and I am a mere social worker. By the way, have either of you reason to suspect that Sadie or

Louella might have attended a party? Is there some sort of common themes as to where the kids are absconding to, do they ever mention anything to the other kids?'

Moira looked completely blank. Lawrence looked steadily at her.

'I can't recall that any of the kids have mentioned anything specifically about parties. Why do you ask?'

Poppy shrugged, thinking back to what David's sister, Tara, had said.

'Oh, it was just a theory I had but it's probably way off beam. Forget I said anything...'


'I'm telling yer I got it from a mate, you can ask her if you want.' Poppy gazed at Sadie's fake tanned, orange complexion, heavy kohled eyes, hoisted up skirt and sighed. Her mousy hair had been bleached and was backcombed and clipped up into an extraordinary bird's nest creation of a hair do. Her school shirt was unbuttoned to reveal the top of her small breasts and she wore a plain scarf round her neck giving her navy and grey school uniform an almost jaunty look. She was slim and lithe and looked rather like a little girl who had been playing around with her mother's makeup. Underneath the false eyelashes, fake tan and heavily pencilled in eyebrows, she was actually a very pretty girl of twelve. It was so sad that she was in such a hurry to grow up. Poppy decided to call her bluff.

'OK, that's fine. I will ask her. What's her name?'

Sadie stared at her defiantly. 'Amy summat or other. I don't know, do I?'

'Well, I will need her surname, address or 'phone number otherwise how will I manage to find her?'

Sadie shrugged her thin shoulders.

'Well, if she's a friend then I expect you will have her 'phone number, won't you?'

Sadie pretended to run a false nail down her contacts.

'Nah, I don't.'

Poppy sighed as she became increasingly exasperated. 'Where were you all weekend? The staff have been worried sick, not to mention your mother who they had to inform, of course. And the police… Anything could have happened to you. Everyone you meet isn't going to be your friend, you know Sadie. Men might take advantage of you, you might be raped or attacked...'

Sadie smirked at the very idea.

'I was wi' Amy I told them.'

'OK, so where did you stay?'

'Just at Amy's mates.'

'Where was that exactly? Was it in York, or in one of the villages?'

Sadie's face took on a bored, shuttered look. 'I dunno, do I? In York or summat. Don't know where 'xactly.'

Poppy realised that she was wasting her time, made some notes in her book and turned the conversation to more neutral topics such as school and friendships. She made a quick note of the type of mobile Sadie had acquired and decided to check out the price later. Sadie was a little more receptive when Poppy left, thinking she had won her battle about the 'phone. As she drove home, her thoughts turned to David Fenton and her conversation with his sister, Tara. Supposing kids were being groomed and sexually exploited by persons unknown? She needed to speak to Andrea as soon as possible and perhaps organise a strategy meeting with the police. Satisfied with that plan, her mind flitted to her visit to Kyle Devlin, and then the pleasant evening she had spent with the jockey Tristan Davies. It was only last week but it felt like a lifetime away. She was almost sorry that she was unlikely to see Tristan again. With Kyle being so settled, there would be no need. Tina was bound to be back at work soon as she was very rarely ill and loved her job. She had to be on her deathbed not to come to work. But somehow, her evening with Tristan had given her a glimpse into other possibilities, other avenues her life might take her, other loves, other friendships and for that she would always be eternally grateful. She no longer felt the need to cling to the wreckage of her broken relationship with Jamie. Not that Jamie had been pleased, of course. In fact, he had been incredulous at first and then furious from the tone of his texts and voicemails. But she felt curiously liberated. She almost wanted to see Tristan again, just so she could thank him.

# Chapter 5

Kyle and Mickey glared at each other.

'First you leave the stable door open, now you've managed to get glass in his bedding. You're nothing but a bloody useless care kid. Go and get your sweet little social worker to kiss you better and hold your hand, eh? You're no good and if I have my way, you'll be down the road!'

Kyle shook his head. 'How many times do I have to tell you, I just came in and found it. I didn't do nothing!'

Tristan and Barry, the Head Lad, moved in between them.

'Pack it in you two.' Barry inclined his head motioning for Mickey to get back to work whilst Tristan calmed Kyle down.

'Come on let's move Bennie and let Mickey see to his fetlock whilst you clear up the bedding, yeah?'

Kyle frowned and led the big bay, Bennie out of his stable into an empty one. The big horse had a slight cut to his fetlock. There was a tiny trickle of blood which Kyle kept anxiously looking at as they walked.

How the hell had that happened? Tristan prodded at the straw bed in Bennie's stable turning it over with his foot. There were several small shards of glass, shining from within the straw. He looked up and saw that the bulb in the light, high up in the roof had shattered. So that was how the glass had got there. Tristan frowned as he looked up at the remaining wizened element. The strange thing was that it was unusual for a light bulb to shatter so completely when it blew. It was possible, but strange nonetheless. Tristan mulled this over. Perhaps, it had been smashed deliberately and there seemed to be far more glass than for one measly light bulb, more like several. Maybe, it looked like more because it had broken into tiny fragments. Something didn't seem to feel quite right, but he was sure that Kyle wasn't to blame. It was just one of those things. Kyle came back looking a little calmer and carried on mucking out.

'Look,' Tristan pointed to the shattered light bulb. 'That's what happened. The light bulb went.'

Kyle sighed. He glanced up at the roof.

'Thank God for that. Tell Mickey will you. He's been on my case all week, as it is.'

Tristan nodded. 'Yeah, no problem. It looks like a tiny nick, I'm sure everything will be fine for tomorrow. Actually, it's lucky really, it could have been so much worse. I'll get Gaz to put another bulb in. And I'll talk to Mickey, no worries.'

Surly Gaz, the handyman, so called for his habitual frown and taciturn manner, grunted a welcome and shuffled into the stable with a ladder and replaced the bulb. He moved silently and miserably about the place, popping up unexpectedly here and there, fixing fences, drains and maintained all the vehicles, including the two horse boxes.

After a short time, Kyle had completely removed all the straw to ensure all the glass splinters were removed and Bennie was happily back in his stable. Mickey had reluctantly agreed the cut was so minor as to be negligible and it seemed as though Tristan's ride tomorrow was back on.

Tristan did manage to have a quiet word with Mickey. 'Just go easy on the kid, right? The light bulb could have gone at any point, it's not his fault.'

'Hmm.' Mickey grunted, but he didn't argue.

'Great, good on you.' Tristan patted his arm, pleased with how well he had taken it. In a way, he thought, it was something of a lost opportunity, though. If things weren't resolved with Kyle and Mickey, then maybe Poppy would have had to come out. He had to admit her was looking forward to seeing her again. He was intrigued by her with her air of sophistication and detachment. She had popped unbidden into his head several times since he had met her. Usually so sure of himself with the opposite sex, something about Poppy made him tongue tied. He would have ordinarily prised her 'phone number out of her in no time, but there was an aura about her that made him hesitate. He really wanted her to like him and not just think he was a jumped up, over sexed jockey. Still, he was pretty sure he would meet her again soon.

Basil Lindley suddenly appeared as he often did, living so close and having a horse in the yard. Basil's horse was a huge, chestnut gelding called In the Pink. He was part of a syndicate and was showing great promise. Basil was a most conscientious owner and was always popping in with carrots and mints for Pinkie, as he was called. Basil always had a cheery word for everyone and was popular with all the lads.

'Just popping by to see how Pinkie is doing.' Basil patted his pocket. 'And give him a carrot or two. Is everything OK? I couldn't help but hear Mickey shouting at that new lad.' Basil frowned with concern. 'If I can help in anyway then do let me, dear boy.'

Tristan looked at Basil's serious hazel eyes.

'Oh, that's very kind of you, but it's something and nothing really. Bennie's stable bulb shattered, and Mickey was blaming Kyle, that's all.'

Basil nodded. 'Well, that could happen to anyone, surely? Was Bennie hurt at all?'

'Well, he has a teensy cut, but nothing really, so there's no harm done.'

Basil visibly relaxed. 'Splendid. Isn't he running tomorrow?'

'Yeah, yeah. He's in the 2.10 at Haydock so he should be fine. I'm hoping for a good run, actually.'

Basil beamed. 'Excellent. Well, the very best of luck to you. Is he worth a flutter, do you think?'

Tristan suspected that Basil wasn't a serious gambler unlike some owners, but was still reluctant to share his real view, which was that he was hoping for a

35

win or at least a place. But then, why not? Basil was such a lovely gentleman in every sense of the word, he was always interested in everyone, a really decent chap.

'He is in great shape, the handicapper has been fair for once, so I'm hoping for a place at least. In fact, you know the mystery tipster in the Yorkshire Bugle, who has been doing really well?' Tristan fished out a crumpled paper from his pocket and pointed at the relevant section. 'Look, Milliman has tipped Bennie to win, so I don't know what odds you'll get...'

Basil winked. 'Milliman, hey? Well, that settles it. Splendid, dear boy. Thanks for the tip.' He tapped the side of his nose.


Tristan had three rides at Haydock the first being aboard Benefactor, or Bennie. He had then been asked to partner Colonel Filbert, a dapple grey in the third and Mission Impossible in the fifth. It was a cold, but sunny November afternoon and the ground was 'good to soft' perfect for an afternoon's racing.

He had travelled ahead in his sporty Audi and was enjoying the banter in the dressing room ahead of his race.

All the talk was of the betting.

'Hey, you're tipped by Milliman in the next,' commented Charlie Durrant, a jockey who Tristan got on well with. 'Do you fancy your chances? Not if I can help it, though. I reckon Molly's Dream can beat you. Easy.'

'In your dreams, more like!'

'Are you on that Colonel Filbert from Tony Reynolds' place?' asked Jake Horton, another confident, cheeky chappie, as he pulled on his boots.

'Yeah, why?'

Jake shook his head. 'Well, good luck, mate. You'll definitely need it. He's a kamikaze ride.' But there was a sparkle in Jake's eyes which suggested that he had no actual knowledge about Colonel Filbert's abilities.

'Yeah right. I don't fancy yours much, either.'

36

Jake grinned and slapped him on the back. 'I had you going there for a minute. You should have seen your face.'

Tristan gave him a wide smile. He loved the camaraderie and piss taking. Being a jump jockey was an incredibly risky and dangerous occupation. The high jinks and laughs were, he guessed, a part of the process of letting off steam. But the thrill of a good race was like no other. He was ready for a great afternoon. All the jockeys seemed in good spirits except for Melvin Clough, an older jockey with a morose personality. When he did speak it was usually to moan about other jockeys, the lack of money in the business or something equally dull. He had weasel like features and a high, whining voice and was regarded as a whinger. Hence, he was not popular with his peers. He glared at Tristan and Jake, unamused by their conversation.

Jake caught the look. 'Cheer up Melvin, it might never happen.'


Jeremy was red and perspiring when he joined him in the parade ring.

'Jesus, what a fiasco! We nearly didn't make it in time. Bloody lorry got a flat tyre and then the spare was missing. Can you believe it! I'll throttle that bloody Gaz. He's paid to maintain the bloody vehicles, not wreck them. Had to get Laura to bring one from the other lorry, but fortunately we weren't too far into the journey.' Jeremy sighed with relief. Then he spotted the owners, a successful builder and his wife, and instantly went on a charm offensive. Tristan smiled at the couple and touched his cap. Tristan had been about to mention the incident with the light bulb but decided that now was not the right time. His mind was working overtime.


Jeremy took him aside for his instructions. 'Try and run him as you usually do. Just take it steady early on, keep to the middle of the field, then use the horse's pace in the last furlong or so. He's going really well so we should be in with a shout. Bennie is a bit unsettled with us rushing, so try and steady him down and then pick them off in the home straight.'

Bennie was slightly sweaty but felt full of life as they cantered up to the start. When the starter's tape went up it was clear that Bennie had other ideas about settling in the middle of the pack. His blood was up, and he was unwilling to respond to Tristan's aids. His jumping was his strong suit and they soared over fence after fence until they were nearly at the front of the field. There was only Melvin riding a dark bay called Apache Summer ahead and with three jumps to go, Tristan allowed Bennie his head as he showed no sign of tiring. Bennie pulled level with Melvin's horse. Melvin glanced at him through his mud spattered goggles and muttered some obscenity that Tristan couldn't quite catch, through the noise of thundering hooves. As they approached the third last, Tristan saw out of the corner of his eye, Melvin manoeuvre the big bay straight towards him. What the hell was he doing? He had plenty of room on the inside. Melvin was tugging at his right rein, mouthing something at him. Adrenaline was coursing through his veins as he came to the inescapable conclusion. There was no doubt in Tristan's mind that Melvin was intending on bringing him down.

Tristan pressed his legs round Bennie urging him on. The horse sprang forward gamely, but not fast enough to avoid a nudge from Apache Summer as he took off over the fence. Unbalanced, Bennie barely cleared the fence, pecking badly on landing. Tristan clung desperately to the saddle and mane, but it was no use. In a split second he was catapulted over Bennie's right shoulder. The ground rushed towards him as he tried to roll and avoid Bennie's hind legs. There was a sickening crunch as he heard his shoulder crack, crippling red hot pain and then it was dark.

The kindly face of the St John's ambulance staff, an older man and a younger one, loomed into view.

'Come on mate, just lay flat whilst we check you out.' Expert hands undid his silks and pronounced on his injuries.

'Think we'll have to take you to hospital, that collarbone does not look good.'

Tristan tried to think about what had happened and managed to croak.

'Is the horse OK?'

The older man chuckled. 'Yeah, plenty of running in him. Some lad just caught him, but he looks fine.'

Well, that was something, he supposed. Later Jeremy and Laura came to pick him up from hospital.

'You poor thing.' Laura frowned. By now Tristan had had several pain killers and the shock was wearing off. He had fractured his right collarbone and a couple of ribs. A month off if he was lucky, six to eight weeks if things didn't heal as well as he expected.

Jeremy patted his back. 'Bad luck. Bennie just pecked on landing, but he's fine, don't worry about a thing. It's not like him though, but there you are. You'll be back in no time.'

Tristan glared at him. Hadn't he seen what happened? Was he blind?

'It was Melvin Clough, he rode into Bennie knocking him off balance just before the fence three from home. Bastard. Didn't you see him?'

Jeremy and Laura were eyeing each other incredulous.

'No, well there was no steward's inquiry.' Laura's voice was soothing.

'And you're bound to get a bit of jostling, Tris,' continued Jeremy smoothly.

Tristan sighed. Bloody Melvin Clough had achieved the impossible. He had managed to bring down Bennie, the red-hot favourite whilst making it look like he was just riding competitively.

'Who won?' he asked in a low voice, but he had already guessed.

Laura patted his hand. 'Oh, Apache Summer, by a few lengths.'

Well, that was no surprise! Rage pulsed through him. This was a set up. First Bennie escaped or was deliberately let out of his stable, then there was glass in his bedding, the lorry had a flat tyre and no spare and then Melvin had managed to barge him out of contention, causing Bennie to fall. It seemed that someone didn't want Bennie to win today. Melvin must be taking a backhander. There had been rumours about him before, but Tristan had never been on the receiving end of it, so had paid no attention. Well, now he was. This was personal, and he vowed whatever it took he would find out who was behind it, because he was sure that Melvin was just the hired help.

Chapter 6

'I'm very worried about Sadie Jones. She has gone missing again this weekend, I assume with the same person or persons as before and The Limes staff suspect she's been drinking and probably using drugs. Last week she came back with a new mobile 'phone that she said she was 'given' by a friend and this week she has new clothes. Louella Simpson was missing at exactly the same time, so I presume they went together, though they don't really get on. I'm very worried about both girls' general safety, but especially Sadie. She's only twelve. She isn't saying anything to us about where she's been and seems to think that the whole matter is a huge joke.'

Andrea tugged at her blonde bob and admired her beautifully manicured fingers.

'Hmm. Well, I agree. It is very concerning. I've just had her mother on complaining. Obviously, the care staff had to inform mum when she went missing. Mrs Jones is stating that she put her daughter in care for her own safety and she's desperately worried. She wants us to consider a secure unit for Sadie.'

Poppy sighed. She supposed Mrs Jones did have a point, even if she had dumped her daughter unceremoniously, complete with two black bin bags, in the office a couple of years ago. She ought, at least, to be safe in care. Still it was a bit rich considering her flimsy reasons for abandoning her daughter. The story was that Sadie and Mrs Jones' new boyfriend were not getting along and the boyfriend had threatened to leave unless Sadie was out of the picture. Poppy was appalled by Mrs Jones' actions. What sort of a woman chose her boyfriend over her then ten year old child? She doubted this boyfriend had stayed the course anyway and Mrs Jones had probably just moved onto another unsuitable bloke. Poor Sadie. She was crying out for attention and love and therefore a perfect target for the unscrupulous. She was also twelve years of age and therefore not able to consent to sexual activity in the eyes of the law. So, any offence against her would be taken very seriously indeed

'So, are you considering it, surely not?'

Andrea shook her head. 'Have you any idea the legal threshold we would have to apply for such an order?' Andrea lifted her hand high above her head, making a chopping motion. 'It's right up here. We would need definitive proof of harm. We would, after all, be depriving her of her liberty. A girl who goes missing for a couple of nights every weekend who to all intents and purposes comes back safe and well, is never going to meet the threshold criteria, despite what Mrs Jones may want. All our concerns are pure speculation. And more to the point, she hasn't made any allegations that she has been harmed.'

Poppy nodded. 'Well, what do you suggest I do with her then?'

'Call a strategy meeting with the police, they may well have more information and undertake some work around good and bad relationships, you know the package you and Katie put together? In fact, why don't you run a group for young girls at The Limes? And we'll take it from there. And keep your ear to the ground. She's bound to let something slip.'

Andrea continued to type up their supervision notes, her fingers dancing on the keyboards. Poppy got up to leave.

'Andrea, did you get the message from Tara Fenton? She sounded very concerned...'

Andrea stopped typing, her eyes never leaving the computer monitor, although the hunch of her shoulders showed signs of definite tension.

'Yes, yes. Thank you.' Then she was off again, fingers going ten to the dozen. Poppy shrugged. It was evident that Andrea didn't want to talk about Tara Fenton or her ramblings. Andrea was usually very professional, but not averse to a teensy bit of gossip from time to time. But it was clear that on this matter, her lips were sealed.


As she arranged her group work session, rang Lawrence Morgan from The Limes to sound him out and suggest a co-worker for the group, she leafed through her messages. To her surprise there was one from Mrs Bloom regarding Kyle Devlin. She rang back straightaway.

'Hi there, it's Poppy Ford here, how can I help you?'

There was a pause as Mrs Bloom considered how to phrase her concerns.

'Well, it may be something and nothing, but Kyle has been acting a bit strangely recently. He seems quite moody, not his usual self, he's bitten our heads off when we've tried to ask him what's wrong. I wonder if it's to do with work, but we can't get any sense out of him. There was an argument at the Trenthams recently and I suspect he is struggling with the other lads. 'Course, you do expect a bit of teasing and so on, but then maybe it's not that. And he was out till very late on Saturday night. Woke us up at about three in the morning, which is way past his bedtime, very drunk. Looked like he'd been in a fight too. He had bruises around his eye and nose. Perhaps, his mother has been in touch or something. Either way, we'd be ever so grateful if you could come out and talk to him. Perhaps, he'll speak to you?'

Poppy wasn't at all sure he would especially as she had only met him once, but it definitely sounded like something was troubling him. She made an arrangement to visit in a couple of days and thought about Kyle. At sixteen, no doubt he was finding it hard to integrate into the world of work. If Mickey's reception was anything to go by then she could see why. Had one of the lads beaten him up? Yet he had seemed into the routine of hard physical work and he clearly loved the horses. Maybe if he had started going out and drinking then he was ready to move on from the Blooms into his own accommodation? Perhaps,

43

she would suggest that to him. The Blooms were a little staid and old fashioned, perhaps, to cope with a teenaged lad with raging hormones and a poor start in life.

Her mobile telephone beeped. It was yet another message from Jamie. Ignoring him had only made him seem much keener. Why hadn't she thought of that before? But she knew that things were really and truly over between them. There was no going back this time. She deleted the message and thought about Tristan. Perhaps, she was going to be able to thank him for helping her put Jamie into perspective after all?

It was a blustery, cold day when she set out for the Trenthams' Yard. She arrived much quicker this time as she knew the route. For a split second she hesitated as she rounded the bend where Bennie had jumped out in front of the car, but thankfully all was clear. There were no stray horses today, just acres of greenery tinged with frost, stretching out ahead of her.

Jeremy came out to greet her. He was in the company of Basil Lindley who bowed slightly and lifted his tweed hat as he saw her. How quaint, she thought, such lovely manners.

'How are you, Poppy wasn't it? Have you come to see Kyle?' asked Jeremy.

'Yes, I did ring Laura, but perhaps if I could just have a word with you first.'

'Yes, yes. Let's have a cuppa. Are you going to join us, Basil?'

Basil inclined his head. 'Well, if it's not too much to ask of dear Laura. I'll just sit and chat to her, or Nelson. I don't want to intrude.'

Poppy nodded. She would have rather had a private chat with Jeremy, but Basil seemed harmless enough.

They followed Jeremy into a room with a large polished table, a Persian rug and horse photographs all over the walls. Laura came in from the kitchen and beamed at Poppy.

'Cup of tea? Or coffee with a nip of something stronger? We've been back from the gallops for at least two hours, but I'm still frozen to the core.' Laura was still wearing her furry headband and her olive padded jacket inside the house. She smiled warmly at Poppy.

'I'll just have a coffee please.'

Poppy glanced at her watch. It was only half past nine. What time did these people get up, she wondered, to have exercised their horses by seven thirty? There were about forty horses in training, she remembered Tristan telling her. So, God knows how long exercising them took.

'No scotch? Are you sure?' Laura managed to sound incredulous.

'Quite sure thanks.'

Basil went to follow Laura into the kitchen.

Jeremy gave her a slow smile. 'So how can I help you?'

'Well, the Blooms have rung me expressing some concerns about Kyle. It may be nothing, but they have noticed he's been a bit short tempered, stayed out late at the weekend, seems to have got into a fight and seems preoccupied. Have you noticed anything unusual, has anything happened that you know of that might have upset him?'

Jeremy frowned. 'I don't think so. He's still working hard and doing well. There was a bit of tension and ribbing from the other lads because of him not closing Bennie's door properly and the incident with the glass. He might have had had some comments from the others, but nothing out of the ordinary. I certainly don't think he's been fighting here. I would take a very dim view of anyone fighting.' Jeremy looked beyond her to the door. 'But Tristan's here now, so let's ask him. He might know more.'

Tristan grinned at her. 'Hi there. How's it going?'

Poppy was annoyed to find that she blushed. How stupid. All she could do was hope that he didn't notice. She nodded at him, taking in the sling on his right arm and his grimace of pain as he sat down.

'Poppy was just saying she had a call from the Blooms with some worries about Kyle. Apparently, he's been moody and off hand, so Poppy was wondering if there's a problem at work. Do you have any ideas?'

Tristan scowled. 'Well, I think he has had a fair bit of stick to do with all the stuff that's been going on with Bennie. I mean if you consider everything that's happened, it looks very dodgy. You know, Bennie being let loose from his stable and the light bulb blowing. Then, there was the problem with the lorry so that Bennie nearly didn't make it to the course, and then we were barged causing us to overbalance and lose the race. He was the red-hot favourite. Probably, the lads think Kyle had something to do with it. I'm sure someone has been trying to nobble Bennie all along and when it didn't work, Clough was paid to finish the job.'

Jeremy smiled weakly, as though humouring a small child. 'Not this again. I think you've been reading too many Dick Francis novels, Tris. Come on, they were all just coincidences, surely? As for Cloughie, that was just a bit of jostling for position, that's all. I know you're injured and annoyed to be out so early in the season, but don't get this out of proportion.'

Poppy looked at Tristan's face. He looked uncomfortable and angry. It was clear to her that Tristan was completely unconvinced by Jeremy's smooth answers. She realised that she was curious to find out exactly what was going on.

# Chapter 7

Kyle certainly seemed rather different. He looked as if he hadn't slept well for days and when he had, it was in his clothes. He seemed twitchy, ill at ease and was certainly spitting feathers about the Blooms ringing up. There were traces of yellowing bruising to his right eye and a graze to his right cheek. Gone were the easy manners and confidence of the boy she had visited two weeks earlier.

'Oh man, I told them not to ring you. Why don't they ever listen? Honestly, there's nothing wrong.'

Poppy nodded unconvinced.

'OK. It's just that you seem restless to me and don't be too hard on the Blooms. They've only got your best interests at heart, you know.'

Kyle ran his grubby fingers through his hair. They were in the same rest room that they had used previously. The Pirelli calendar was still in evidence and a couple of notices and adverts were pinned to the notice board. Kyle fumbled with the gas heater which spluttered into life. It was going to take a while for the room to warm up, Poppy realised edging nearer to the heater. She remembered the overwhelming smell of the leather. She wondered how to tackle Kyle and opted for a direct approach.

'You seem out of sorts and uptight, Kyle. How did you get those bruises? Have you been in a fight? What's going on?' Kyle's face was immobile, and he had difficulty meeting her eye.

She tried again, this time a different tack.

'So, have you seen anything of your parents recently?'

Kyle shrugged his shoulders. 'Yeah. I bumped into me mum.'

'OK.' Poppy tried to read his body language. Was there a flicker of annoyance or had she imagined it? 'So, was everything alright when you last saw your mum, did she say anything to upset you?'

Kyle shrugged again. 'Nah, she's pretty annoying. Always was, always will be.'

Kyle flicked the switch on the grubby white kettle and fished around for tea bags.

'Do you wanna drink?'

Poppy shook her head, again studying him for clues.

'So, you were out late on Saturday night, I hear. Did you get into a fight? Came back drunk, didn't you? Were you out with someone, a girlfriend for example?'

There was a flicker of something that passed over Kyle's face, a flash of emotion before his face reverted to its set expression.

'Nah, just fell over that's what happened. And no girlfriend. Fancy free, that's what I am.' There was a trace of bitterness in his voice. Poppy thought he looked anything but 'fancy free'. He looked weighed down by something.

'OK, so who were you out with?'

'Oh, just some of me mates.'

Poppy nodded again and watched him as he gulped back his tea.

'Anyone from here?'

'Nah.'

Poppy remembered what Jeremy had said about the lads getting on his case about Bennie's recent mishaps.

'Do you get on alright with the lads here, only Jeremy, Mr Trentham said there had been some problem to do the them blaming you about Bennie.'

Kyle looked steadily at Poppy. 'Yeah. It's all sorted now though. The lads were getting on at me. But he fell in his race and it weren't me riding him, so they can't blame me for that, can they?'

Poppy took this in but couldn't help feel that she had given him the explanation and he had gone along with it. 'So, you've taken a bit of ribbing, have you? What sort of things have they said?'

Kyle shook his head. 'Oh, just some crap, or other. It's alright now, though.'

'OK. Well just remember if you have a problem, you can ring my mobile or if it's out of hours the Emergency Duty Team number. That's what we're here for.'

As she left, she passed the Pirelli calendar fascinated by the big busted beauties laying provocatively over vehicles. What sort of woman would demean herself to do that? It was then that she noticed a small pale pink card pinned to the notice board, edged with gold.

*ss Modelling Agency and Professional Photography. Have you got what it takes to be a top model? Make millions and travel the world. Expert advice given. For your free portfolio contact 07766554433 or contact us on twitter @bossmodels*

ss Modelling Agency. It was certainly a strange name. She had an image of the SS, Nazi storm troopers, preening themselves for the camera. She shook her head to rid herself of the uncomfortable image. Then she realised that the top corner of the card had been torn off leaving the 'ss' bit. It looked out of place next to the other ads for hay, box drivers and work riders. How very strange. She wondered what the full name was? The world of modelling and horse racing did not seem at all related. But what did she know? She copied down the wording in her big diary word for word without knowing why. It might be important. She left the room, deep in thought. Tristan was hovering in the tack room fiddling with a bridle as she came out with Kyle. He watched as Kyle picked up his pitchfork and moved off continuing his work.

'Any joy?'

'Well, from what I have gathered he took some teasing from the other lads, but he says it's fine now. And as for his injuries he said he fell over.'

Tristan grinned. 'But you don't believe him?'

Poppy nodded acknowledging it to herself. 'No, I'm not sure I do.'

Tristan glanced at his watch. 'Listen. Do you fancy a chat? Got time for elevenses or an early lunch in The Yew Tree?'

Poppy nodded. She had a meeting later that afternoon and heaps of paperwork to do but she could spare an hour or so. She had to eat.

'Yeah, OK.'

Tristan nodded, pleased. 'Let me just change the bit on this bridle and I'll be right with you.'

Poppy was surprised by Tristan's smart Audi sports car. She didn't know how much jockeys earned, but someone starting out in their career like Tristan, she decided, would not earn a lot. She also wasn't at all sure he should be driving with his injury and said as much.

Tristan merely smiled. 'It's only down the road, it'll be fine. I've had loads of fractures. It's sort of an occupational hazard.' Poppy did notice him trying to disguise his pain when he steered. Thankfully, the injuries were to his right side otherwise he couldn't change gear. The car was quite luxurious inside. It certainly made a change from her old Renault. Tristan explained that as a stable jockey for the yard he rode most of the horses but was free to take other rides from other stables as long as the Trenthams didn't have a runner.

'So, I need a decent car to get to all these race meetings,' he explained. 'But I could do without this damned injury, at the start of the season too.'

They made their way to The Yew Tree which displayed a full lunch menu and a vast range of cakes. They ordered baguettes, chips and a pot of tea.

50

'So, what's been going on with Kyle?' asked Tristan. Even he seemed out of sorts and less comfortable than when she last met him. His face looked grey and he was clearly in a lot of pain. There was something else. She sensed anger and a rugged determination.

'Well, the foster carers rang me as he seemed out of sorts, irritable, unsettled and he went out and came back at three in the morning blind drunk. He also looks like he's been in a fight. So, I am concerned.'

Tristan nodded. 'What do you think has happened?'

Poppy shook her head. 'I'm not sure but he seemed really down but brushed it all off. He says the other lads were getting on at him about Bennie. I'm not sure if this went so far as to cause the fight but then he feels like he's off the hook with him falling in the race anyway.'

Tristan nodded grimly, not wanting to be reminded.

'So how long will you be off?'

'Oh, 'bout a month or so.'

Poppy nodded. She was sure fractures would take at least six weeks to heal. Were all jockeys completely mad?

'So, what was all that about with Jeremy earlier?'

Tristan frowned. 'Well, I think there is a problem in the yard, and it could affect Kyle too.' Tristan looked at her steadily. 'Let me just run this past you. Firstly, Bennie is let out of his stable, then there's glass found in his bedding supposedly from a smashed light bulb. This causes a minor cut, but neither is enough to stop him running. Are you with me so far?' Poppy nodded. 'But there's more. Bennie nearly didn't get to Haydock as the lorry had a flat tyre and no spare. I'm sure that spare was removed in order to prevent him getting there. They only made it because Laura was able to bring another tyre from the other lorry. And then to cap it all, I was cut up very badly by Melvin Clough who rode the eventual winner, who was a 10-1 longshot. He rode his horse into Bennie unbalancing him, and causing him to stumble and me to fall, I'm sure of it.' Tristan's face flushed with anger. 'So, the lads are suspicious and think Kyle may be involved.'

'Surely there are rules about riding into other people, aren't there? You could have been killed.' Poppy was appalled.

Tristan gave her a rueful smile. 'Well, that's just it. Neither the stewards or anyone else thought it was out of order, but believe me, someone paid Clough to barge into me and Bennie and I'm sure they tried to nobble him so that the rank outsider, Apache Summer romped home.'

Poppy's mind was in a whirl. She knew nothing about racing, but it certainly sounded suspicious. If the other lads suspected Kyle of being involved, they may have taken it out on him.

'If what you're saying is true then whoever organised it must have had an insider to open the stable door, sprinkle the glass, remove the spare tyre and so on. And whoever that is might be feeling remorseful and unsettled. There may have been a change in their behaviour too, like with Kyle?'

Tristan nodded. 'Well, it's possible and the lads must think so too. After all, it's natural to blame a newcomer. Everyone else has been here for a lot longer than Kyle.'

Poppy tried to take this in. Kyle involved in nobbling horses? Surely not? She suddenly felt ill equipped to deal with this. This world of racing was completely alien to her, she realised.

'But if Kyle is involved then he will have been put up to it.' Tristan grimaced.

'Do you think he is?' Suddenly it was really important to know what Tristan was really thinking.

Tristan shook his head, as though weighing everything up. 'No, I don't. And I reckon he's had enough crap in his life already. I'm keen to prove he isn't involved. If things escalate and the guvnor starts to listen to the lads, then he'll sack him without hesitation. So, the sooner we can prove his innocence the better.'

Poppy thought about how enthusiastic Kyle was at their initial meeting and his hopes about becoming a jockey. From what she had heard, he had a good chance of making it. This would do irreparable damage to him. She noticed the 'we' bit.

'OK. How can I help?'

# Chapter 8

Tristan considered his options. With no-one except him and now possibly Poppy taking these allegations seriously it was difficult to make progress. His best plan, he figured, was to carry on, smile sweetly and do some digging behind the scenes in the hope that he could find something useful out. So, he couldn't ride for a bit, but he still helped out in the yard and with his ice baths and some of Mickey's comfrey oil, he was banking on being back in work in no time. Although, he hated missing out on racing, this did give him some time to find out what the hell was going on. First off, he would start with Melvin Clough and see what a visit to him might reveal. He scoured the Racing Post for information as to where Melvin was racing next, and took himself off to Market Rasen Races, where Melvin had a few rides. As he left his cottage, he put his hands in his jacket pocket and felt his penknife. He used it for cutting open bales of hay or straw or feed sacks. He was going to remove it but decided against it. He had no idea what he was getting involved in and it might just pay to have a weapon of sorts.

It was a chilly November day, but the clouds started to clear a little as he drove the short distance to Market Rasen racecourse. The pain from his ribs and collarbone were numbed by the painkillers he had taken, and he began to enjoy the drive. He arrived at the course, flashed his ID and gained access to the car park where the jockeys usually parked. He continued to read his Racing Post whilst keeping an eye out for Clough's arrival. He had a runner in the first, so he figured he didn't have long to wait. Sure enough, after about ten minutes or so, he spotted Clough arriving alone in his silver VW Golf. The car park was deserted so Tristan ran forward towards the exit and met Clough head on as he rounded the corner into the main courtyard. Clough looked surprised, as recognition dawned. He gave Tristan a weak smile. His face soon fell as he caught the look on Tristan's face. Clough glanced around nervously, as if looking for someone that might help.

He began to gabble. 'Now then mate. Didn't know you were racing today. Thought you were off for a bit, what with the fall and that...'

Tristan continued to glare at him. The 'mate' part had really rankled with him. He was never going to be Clough's mate, never. He struggled to keep a lid on his temper. Clough swallowed nervously.

'Now cut the crap, Melvin. You and I both know you were out of order last week at Haydock. Is that how you get by these days? Quite an art, isn't it managing to barge someone without anyone else noticing and avoiding a Steward's Inquiry? The connections must have been delighted with a win at 10-1, mustn't they?'

Melvin continued to walk on. 'Don't know what you're on about Tris, mate. You must still be concussed or paranoid.'

With his good arm, Tristan grabbed Melvin's collar. 'Now just you tell whoever paid you off that I'm on to them. I'm gonna find out who put you up to it and get the accomplice who tried to stop Bennie running. Who let Bennie out of his stable and then put glass in his bedding, not to mention removing the spare tyre on the lorry? Who?'

Melvin looked flustered. 'I don't know what you're talking about.'

As he struggled from Tristan's grip, his weasel like face had paled. He was smaller and less muscular than Tristan. Tris pulled himself to his full height and let him go, causing him to almost fall to the ground. He scrambled to his feet. Tristan was almost tempted to kick him for good measure but decided against it. He needed to keep his cool, so he could find out the Mr Big in the operation not merely the hired help.

'Whoever it is, tell them I'm coming for them.' Melvin's shoulders stiffened and then he slowed imperceptibly before looking back at Tristan. The look was a curious mixture of bravado tinged with fear.

Tristan tried to settle down for an afternoon's racing, nodding here and there at people he knew. His mind was in turmoil. After the second race he made his way to the bookies' pitches and had a word with a couple of guys he knew from way back. Having had a cursory glance at the race card and a glimpse at the runners in the parade ring, he picked out a likely bay mare, Inca Princess and approached Graham Kent. In his stable lad days, Tristan had not been averse to betting until he realised that bookies are usually on the winning side. These days he regarded betting as a mug's game but when he had gambled, he had often used Graham who was a decent sort.

'Now then, Tristan, how are you, my son.' Graham Kent was a short, squat man with a wide smile showing several gold teeth. He gave Tristan an appraising look. 'Not racing today then I take it?'

Tristan have him a rueful smile. 'Nah, had a fall last week at Haydock. I'll be back soon though.'

Graham eyes narrowed. 'Ah, yes, so you did with Benefactor who was odds on favourite. We had to pay out on Apache Summer who came in at 10-1, didn't we?' Tristan grinned back. Trust a bookie to remember the losses. Perhaps, he would remember the punters who were involved too?

'Yeah, that's right. Any information about who bet on the winner, Apache Summer? '

Graham quickly took another bet and then narrowed his eyes as he thought.

'Course, it's all confidential like, ain't it?'

'Certainly is, I just wondered that's all.'

Graham gave him a sorrowful look. 'All bets are paid out, now though. You ain't got an inkling it weren't legit, have yer?'

Tristan shook his head. 'Nah, it was just a stupid fall that was all. It was my pride that was hurt mainly.'

Graham laughed and clapped Tristan on the back. 'Well, I took a couple of bets off Niall Devlin who was well pleased with himself when Apache Summer came in. He had a treble with another couple of winners. Did quite well. Don't think there were many big bets, though, otherwise the odds would've shortened.'

Niall Devlin. Kyle Devlin. Tristan nodded trying to avoid betraying too much interest. Could he and Kyle be related?

'What was the bet, can you recall?'

Graham flicked through his ledger. 'A nifty, old son.'

Tristan gave him a quizzical look.

'£50 quid, to you.'

'What were the other horses in the bet?'

Graham consulted his ledger. 'Kerrystone in the 3.15 at Uttoxeter and Halcyon Days in the 4.50 at Market Rasen.'

Tristan nodded committing these names to memory. 'Any idea who Niall works for these days?'

'Nah, not sure mate.' Graham began working through his queue of punters as the time of the next race approached. Tristan placed an each way bet on Inca Princess and moved on.

'Cheers, Graham. You've been very helpful.'

Graham nodded and gave him a wink.


Tristan watched the jockeys mount and kept a close eye on Melvin Clough who was riding another outsider, Testimony. He was joined in the parade ring by trainer Eddie Curran and a middle aged, distinguished looking man, his younger, very attractive partner and two younger men who he guessed were the owner's sons. They looked similar in age to the new girlfriend or wife whose long legs and perfect figure would not be out of place on a catwalk. She hung on to the older man's arm, in a manner that made him dismiss the idea that she was his daughter. The gesture was far too intimate. Tristan glanced at his race card and checked the owner out. **Luca Manfredi.** Tristan committed this to memory. The sons were mini versions of their father, a similar age to Tristan, dressed impeccably in grey suits, overcoats and sunglasses. Tristan's eyes were drawn to the stunning brunette whose perfect figure was encased in a red, woollen dress, high heeled black boots, a black felt hat and black jacket. Then he noticed a familiar face. Niall Devlin, one time jump jockey who had been warned off due to illegal betting. He was a square, thickset man who had clearly piled on the pounds since his jockeying days. His bright blue eyes and busted nose were easily recognisable under his formal dress. He wandered into the ring and whispered in Luca's ear. Then he was gone.

Clough's mount Testimony came in second at 12-1 narrowly beating Inca Princess by a short head. The favourite Tally Ho romped home to win. Tristan was glad he'd had an each way bet, collected his winnings, had a bite to eat and headed off home none the wiser.

As he drove back, he reviewed his progress. OK, he felt some satisfaction from confronting Melvin Clough, but he hadn't really gained any useful information otherwise. Niall Devlin had had a bet on Apache Summer and two other horses in a treble, but it was a small one in betting terms and wouldn't be enough to justify going to the trouble of nobbling Benefactor. Niall Devlin looked to be employed by Luca Manfredi, but again so what? He vowed to undertake some research back at the cottage. He had pegged Niall Devlin as a relative of Kyle's and wondered if Niall had used his influence to persuade Kyle to ruin Bennie's chances? After all, Niall did have form. He could be way off beam. He may not be even be related. If so, what did it prove? He realised it meant nothing. He just hoped that Poppy had had better luck.

All the procedures for kids missing from care were being pursued. This meant that a Senior staff member spoke to both Louella and Sadie about their whereabouts. The two had gone missing over the weekend, but only on the Saturday night. They came back cocky and full of it later on Sunday in time for school on Monday. Helen Sykes, the senior social worker who had formally interviewed the girls, rang Poppy to explain about her interview with them.

'This is turning out to be very odd. Sadie gave a similar version of events to the one she told you. Simply that she spent time with her mysterious friend, Amy. Amy doesn't have a surname or address according to Sadie. Can you check out whether there is someone in Sadie's class called Amy and get any information you can about her.'

'Yes, yes that's no problem. Any information on Louella? Do you think they were together?'

Helen paused. 'Well, this is where it gets interesting. Louella also says she was staying with a friend, called Charlotte, but doesn't know where she lives or her surname either. The interesting thing is that staff here believe she was going out with a young man in foster care aged about 16, but now she has been heard to talk about this lad being a 'boy' and hints about meeting older, more exciting males. So, she could be meeting an older man. She spends ages on her appearance apparently and seems to have acquired a range of new clothing, all of it skimpy and quite revealing. So, even though they came back I am worried that Louella and Sadie are disappearing together and could in the process of being groomed.'

Poppy took this in. 'What was the name of the lad in foster care that Louella was seeing?'

Helen paused as she checked. 'It's Kyle, Kyle Devlin.'

Chapter 9

'So, do we have any leads about where Sadie and Louella are going? Do they disappear together, do they communicate with each other within the home or give any indication that they have spent time together? Do they have any in jokes or codes that they may use?'

The meeting had been convened at short notice to consider the safety of both Sadie and Louella who had absconded from the unit now on four different occasions. Both had come back with expensive items at different times such as mobiles and clothes. Both were refusing to say where they had been and had given vague details of who had accompanied them. They appeared tired and were suspected of drinking and possibly taking soft drugs but were otherwise unharmed. None of the information they had given could be confirmed. The meeting involved schools, the residential staff, social workers and specialist members of the police, trained in the sexual exploitation of vulnerable young people. It was chaired by Helen Sykes, a Senior Social Worker.

Lawrence Morgan consulted his notes. 'I have read every diary sheet that staff have completed and interviewed each staff member separately about the girls. I can find no links at all between them. In fact, I would say they tend to stay away from each other. Possibly this is deliberate, but the only thing so far that they have in common is the pattern of their absconding.'

Helen nodded and invited other agencies to give their information. Sadie's teacher, Mrs Fountain described Sadie as 'immature and difficult'.

'In fact, I must say that despite her Personal Education Plan and support from all the agencies, she is in danger of being permanently excluded. She was in isolation for three days last week and as soon as she returned to the class then she was persistently disruptive and assaulted another pupil resulting in her being excluded again for three days.'

Poppy gaped at the mention of permanent exclusion. She hadn't been aware of that. Helen Sykes was also concerned.

'I'm not sure permanent exclusion is the answer here.'

Mrs Fountain pursed her lips. 'Well, it is a matter of course for the head teacher. But, can I just say we have other children to consider and their education is being badly disrupted.'

'OK. Has Sadie said anything to any staff member about her activities, for example has she been bragging about where she got her mobile telephone.'

Mrs Fountain consulted her notes detailing Sadie's misdemeanours. 'On the 15th of November she had her mobile confiscated as she was constantly using it in lessons. She became very distressed and said that 'the boss would be angry.' She was told she could have it back at the end of the day and did manage to stay in class and collect it later. That's it really.'

'Who do you think she was referring to? Who is 'the boss', do you think?'

Mrs Fountain flushed. 'I'm afraid I can't say, I'm just reading from the notes and wasn't present at the time, you understand.'

Poppy took this in. She wrote 'the boss' in her notes and underlined it three times. Then Helen moved on to ask Poppy about her involvement. She outlined the information regarding her unproductive meeting with Sadie.

'She referred to that fact that she was staying with a friend called Amy. This later changed to staying at a mate of Amy's. She claimed not to know Amy's surname nor details of the friend's address, just that it was in York. She was very evasive to say the least.'

Helen listened intently and made notes. 'Mrs Fountain, can I ask you if Sadie associates with any girls called Amy at school?'

Mrs Fountain screwed up her face. 'Well, of course, Amy is a common name. There are several Amy's in Sadie's class, but I must say they certainly don't spend any time with Sadie and wouldn't have anything in common at all.' Mrs Fountain disapproval of Sadie was all too obvious.

There was a similar discussion regarding Louella. Louella had, it seemed been a bit more vocal, but this was in relation to her splitting up with Kyle Devlin. Still she had made her views plain to staff at the Children's Home.

'Louella told me that Kyle was a bit too young for her and she liked more mature men who would spoil her, spend money on her and who had cars. She referred to Kyle as a 'baby' and as 'wet behind the ears' but when I asked her if she had met anyone else that might be more suitable, she shut down and refused to say anything else. When asked where she had been each time she disappeared, she claimed to have spent the evening with friends at a party but couldn't give an address or full details of the friends.'

'Hmm.' Helen looked thoughtful. 'Has anyone spoken to Kyle about Louella? Perhaps, if he's been spurned, he may be prepared to give us a bit more information?'

Poppy decided to chip in. 'I am covering Kyle Devlin's case whilst his worker is off. He's currently working at a racing yard in Walton, so I could call in and ask him, if you think it would help?'

Helen beamed. 'That would be marvellous, Poppy, thanks. We have to at least try to cover all bases. We really don't have anything much to go on at the moment.' She glanced at a plain clothes policeman from the Public Protection Team. 'DC Spencer, do you have any information that could help us?'

'Not really. I am happy to run checks on any males the girls are associating with to see if they are known to us. Of course, we have been out and conducted searches when the girls have been reported missing, but we've been unable to find them from the information we've been given and then they have returned the next day seemingly unharmed in any event. That's all I can say.'

Helen scribbled in her notebook and went through her recommendations.

'In view of the lack of information, can I suggest that Poppy visit Kyle and ask him if he has any information on Louella's associates and we all monitor the situation closely. As we are all aware sexual exploitation, especially in the early stages can take the form of lots of grooming and this may be what we're seeing here. We'll convene another meeting in about a month's time? How does that sound?'

The group began flicking through their diaries, as Helen and her minute taker went through possible dates. Helen has articulated Poppy's thoughts exactly. They hadn't come up with anything concrete. Poppy couldn't help feeling that they were missing something obvious. It was as though the truth was just ahead but tantalisingly out of reach, like a vivid dream that fades upon waking. Poppy's thoughts chased round and round trying to resolve the puzzle, but to no avail.


Andrea appeared very stressed, Poppy couldn't help but notice. She seemed a completely different person these days. Even her comments about attractive men had ground to her a halt, she had much less time for chatting with her staff and wore a permanent frown. Her office door, which was invariably propped open was now usually closed and she emerged rarely and only to make a drink, avoiding eye contact with the team. She was focused solely on work. Probably, it was due to an impending inspection. You never knew when Ofsted might decide to turn up, but Poppy suspected it was more than that.

Poppy was doing duty again and there was only one other worker in. Maureen, Phil and Jamie were out on visits and Katie was on her way out too.

'Wish me luck, then. I'm off to try and persuade the Kendalls to give Chanelle another chance. Honestly, she is a teenager and she is exhibiting teenage behaviour so I'm not sure what they expect from her? Still, I'll try and work my charm on them and Chanelle, of course.'

Poppy grinned. The Kendalls were foster carers who generally specialised in teenagers, unlike many. However, even they were getting fed up with Chanelle's antics.

'I'm sure you will manage to turn things round, read Chanelle the riot act otherwise she'll end up in at The Limes and things are not too good there with kids going missing and so on.'

'Yeah, I heard about that. How was the strategy meeting? Did you find anything out?'

Poppy shook her head. 'Not really. The girls turn up right as rain the next day, none of their stories check out about where they've been, and the police can't really do anything because we have nothing to go on, no males or addresses to check out.'

Katie looked thoughtful, her dark eyes serious. She had been qualified for years and had so much experience, it was really useful to run things past her. She had previously worked in a specialist unit for teenagers who were frequent absconders. Several had been lured into prostitution in Manchester whilst on the run. Poppy shuddered at the thought of this happening to Louella or Sadie.

'Don't leave any stone unturned on this one. My experience working with runaways is that they can easily get hooked in by criminal gangs. They start off so subtly by giving them drink and gifts moving on to drugs. Suddenly they find they are hooked and need to turn a few tricks for these so called 'boyfriends' who turn into 'pimps'. Listen very carefully to what the girls are saying. There will be some clues. Anyway, must dash.'

'Thanks, Katie. I will keep listening. Good luck with Chanelle.'

Poppy continued to write up her case notes when another duty call was put through.

'Hello, Poppy Ford here, how can I help?'

'I need to speak wi' Andrea…'

The voice was slurred and barely audible.

'Fine. Can I ask who's calling?'

'Tara, Tara Fenton.'

Poppy tried to put the call through, but Andrea's line was engaged.

'Sorry. Andrea is on another call, but I can take a message. Is there anything I can help you with, or shall I put you on hold or ask her to ring you back?'

Tara sighed and then she heard a strangled sob. 'No, no, I never, boss. I'm on a call to the social 'bout my money...That's what this it...No!' There was muttering from someone else, a scuffle and then a piercing scream, followed by terrified sobbing. Then the line went dead.

'Tara, Tara are you there? What's happening, are you in trouble?' But there was no reply. Poppy rang reception to see if they could give her the number Tara was ringing from. It was a mobile. She tried to ring back but there was no-one picking up. It rang and rang.

Poppy felt a wave of fear wash over her. Supposing Tara had been attacked? Clearly, someone had frightened her and why was she having to lie about ringing up? Supposing she did have information about David's death? She remembered their previous conversation. She couldn't just leave it, after what she had just heard. She dialled Andrea's extension and realised that she was still on a call. Feeling that she had no choice, she rang 999 to report the incident and just hoped that the police could trace Tara's mobile to the location. She just hoped that she wasn't too late.

Chapter 10

Tristan's shoulder and rib injuries were making reasonable progress thanks to a regime of ice packs and Mickey's comfrey oil. This was brewed by Mickey from comfrey root, but the actual recipe was a secret known only to him and had been passed down from his father and grandfather before him. Whatever was in the dark green mixture, it definitely accelerated healing. Tristan had seen the results with the horses, so was keen to try it. He was itching to ride and decided to ask Jeremy if he could go out on the gallops. Surely, it wouldn't hurt? Unfortunately, Jeremy had other ideas.

Jeremy was emphatic. 'Absolutely no, Tris. Look. I want you back as our stable jockey, but there's no point in rushing these things. If you fall off, then it could be even worse for you. You jump jockeys are all the same. Tough as old boots. But you've just got to be patient. It's been barely a week for Christ's sake!'

Tris sighed. 'But I'll be fine, you know that. It's 100% better, I swear.'

Jeremy was adamant. Tristan noticed the set of his jaw and decided against pushing it. Laura gave him a sympathetic look.

'Why don't you try the next best thing and supervise some of the newer stable lads who need to do some schooling? Why not take Kyle and Socks?'

Jeremy was delighted. 'A wonderful idea, Laura. Well, what are you waiting for?'

Tristan pulled a face. He was thoroughly bored and desperate to get back into the saddle, but he also knew when he was beaten. Anyway, it would give him a chance to get to know Kyle and perhaps it would help him find out who was behind nobbling Bennie. His other lines of inquiry had come to nothing.

Tristan had googled Luca Manfredi and found everything that you'd expect, namely that he was a wealthy man with a range of businesses including property. He had found out that Niall Devlin's treble winners had all had reasonable odds, so he figured he would have done pretty well out of it. But with a £50 stake, it certainly wasn't big bucks and definitely wasn't worth the bother or the risk of causing Bennie to fall. His head hurt just thinking about it and he certainly needed the distraction. He knew he wasn't wrong about his suspicions, but proving it was altogether a different matter. He found Kyle sweeping up.

'Right. Kyle. Let's take Socks into the bottom paddock and do some schooling. The rest of you can go up to the gallops as usual.'

Mickey and Graeme, one of the other lads, scowled at Kyle as if envious of him being singled out for special treatment. Tristan noticed this immediately and worried that this might incite further tensions.

'Guvnor's orders,' he added, hoping to quell any grumbling.

Kyle quickly saddled up the chestnut with four white socks, hence the stable name Socks, and mounted. He looked small and nervous as he sat on the large horse. Socks had won a few races as a two and three year old on the flat, but had the scope and power to go over hurdles. However, he was still a little green jumping. Tristan had previously schooled him and felt he could do very well.

As they made their way down to the paddock with three flights of brush hurdles, he noticed the tension in Kyle's shoulders. He knew that Jeremy had taught him the rudiments of riding and he was perfectly capable of racing on the gallops, but he wasn't sure that if this included jumping over fences.

'Have you done much jumping, Kyle? Are you ready to give it a go?'

'Yeah, I'll do my best. I haven't done much but reckon you can teach me.'

Tristan nodded, liking his attitude. 'I certainly can.'

Tristan liked to school horses properly and had Kyle circling nicely in trot and canter before attempting any of the obstacles.

'That's right. Let's get him balanced and settled. Just adjust that left rein, that's it.' When he was satisfied, Tristan pointed to a wide log. 'Let's see you go over the log, before we take on anything else. Remember to widen your hands to prevent him running out and move your weight forward as you approach the fence. Give him his head, the worst thing is if you're not quick enough and he gets a jab in the mouth. That will definitely put him off.'

Kyle circled and set off in a canter towards the log. Socks flew over, but Kyle was a little slower to adjust his balance and wobbled dangerously.

'Not bad, but just try it again and remember to move your body forward as you approach the log. OK?'

Kyle circled again and made a much better shape over the fence. However, Socks buoyed up grabbed the bit between his teeth and galloped on, enjoying the freedom.

'Turn him round,' Tristan shouted. 'Come on, don't let him get away with that behaviour. He's just being cheeky.'

He watched as the lad struggled but managed to turn and settled Socks round into a circle again.

'Well ridden. Come on, go again.'

This time Kyle and Socks performed perfectly. Tristan caught up with Kyle who was looking much more settled and confident.

'Well done. Do you fancy having a go at the hurdles?'

Kyle nodded. 'Great, can't wait.'

'OK. Just take it steady remember to rebalance your weight and think about the striding.' Tristan paced out the distance between the fences. 'He's a big horse so you want to be taking off about here, or thereabouts.' Tristan dug his heel into the turf a few feet away from the fence. 'Got it?'

As he waited for Kyle, Tristan's eyes were drawn to a small shimmering light near the hedge toward the boundary. The lights glinted, and he suddenly had a clear view. Binoculars, Tristan realised, running up toward the hedge. Who the hell was it? As he approached, he heard the squeal of brakes as a large silver vehicle drove off, speeding around the corner. Spies. Damn. They must have spotted him approaching. He didn't even catch the number plate. As he turned back, he was just in time to see Kyle and Socks clear the last hurdle in perfect style.

'Go again, sorry I was a bit distracted there. But it looked good.'

Kyle soared over the fences again effortlessly.

Kyle was grinning from ear to ear. Tristan could really relate to that reaction. That's what fuelled him, the feeling of a powerful beast beneath him as he soared high over the fences. The adrenaline rush on a good day was like no other. There were bad days of course and every jump jockey knew that a bad mistake could end your career or even your life. But it didn't do to dwell on this.

Tristan took in Kyle's flushed cheeks and the sparkle in his eyes. He knew that he was feeling it too.

'Well done. You definitely have potential.' He took in Kyle's slim frame and height. 'You could train to be a jump jockey, you know, provided you don't grow too much in terms of height and build. Parents small, are they?'

Then he remembered Kyle's circumstances and could have kicked himself. Typically, he realised, he had just put his size 9 feet straight in it.

Kyle's blue eyes studied him, and he said with quiet dignity. 'Mum is short, and dad is too. Least, I think so.'

Tristan nodded He kept his tone light.

'Do you see them much?'

Kyle's face had clouded. 'My mum, yeah. Not me dad. Not if I can help it. I hate him.' There clearly wasn't much love lost there and there was no mistaking the bitterness in Kyle's voice. His buoyant mood had instantly evaporated.

Tristan nodded, not sure what to say as they made their way back to the stable. He mulled things over. Who had been watching them schooling? It was not unusual for yards to be targeted by watchers in search of betting tips, but Tristan had never known this happen before at the Trenthams. Why were they there now?

Tristan watched all manner of emotions flicker over Kyle's face as he unsaddled Socks. There was no mistaking the anguish that Tristan's questions had provoked. Tristan felt guilty at destroying his excitement. He wished Poppy was there to smooth things over. Hell, he actually felt sorry for the lad. He must be getting soft in his old age. He was keen to leave things on a more positive footing but struggled with the right words to say. His own family weren't rich or educated, but they had muddled through and he had had an abundance of love and security. His parents were always supportive of his dreams and ambitions even if they didn't quite understand them. It was enough that they were his goals for them to become their goals. He couldn't imagine what it must be like without that. He found he really wanted to help. But he needed to trust Kyle implicitly. Perhaps, rather than soothing words, it was time for even more plain speaking.

He met Kyle's gaze. 'Good job today. I'll speak to the guvnor about further schooling and who knows? Maybe, you could get a conditional licence in the future. It's bloody hard work and far from glamorous. But I'm definitely not going to waste my time with someone who isn't 100% honest. Do you understand? So, think very carefully about how you answer my next question.'

Kyle nodded.

'Were you involved in those incidents with Bennie?'

Kyle's gaze was unwavering. 'No.'

'Sure?'

'Of course, I'm sure and I won't let you down.'

'If I find out you were involved, I could make things very difficult for you. In fact, one word from me and you'll be down the road.'

Tristan looked at the young face with the cobalt eyes and soft curls. He reckoned himself to be a good judge of character, he'd never been wrong yet. And he believed him. So, if Kyle wasn't involved then who the hell was?

Chapter 11


It was the weekend and Poppy had been invited to her grandparents for Sunday lunch.

'Do bring that nice boyfriend, if he can make it,' Millicent had added. Poppy had merely made some excuse or other which seemed to satisfy her grandmother. The other girls in the house she shared, a terraced property overlooking the racecourse in York, were either away or with boyfriends so she was kicking her heels a little. She didn't regret not letting Jamie back into her life, but in her free time she did miss him or rather doing couple like things, she had to admit. Her younger brother, Dan, was no doubt living it up at the University of Hull, where he was studying computing or programming or something equally impenetrable. A laconic, spotty youth with his fingers constantly flitting over a computer keyboard, he had worried everyone with his ability to hack into IT systems, once being reprimanded by the police for a minor infringement of the school's IT system. He had matured into an interesting young man and was hoping to turn his skills into a career. She had gone with mum to settle him into the landscaped halls of residence, called the Lawns, and later they had had a trip into Hull. She had been surprised to find the Marina beautiful and full of character, a mix of new and old with some delightful, historic streets which boasted of its rich maritime history. The backdrop of the Humber Bridge, which straddled the Humber estuary between the East Riding and Lincolnshire, was an impressive structure that never ceased to amaze her.

She would have loved to talk over her feelings with Mum, but she was away on a business trip to Mexico sourcing materials for her jewellery business. Poppy's parents had divorced when she was small. Her mother, an educated, creative woman had decided to make the best of it and set up an online jewellery business, specialising in silver and gemstones which from very small beginnings had flourished into a large company. Her mother lived in a large farmhouse set in five acres in rural Yorkshire with a large workshop. Alchemy as the business was known, was thriving, but her mother never lost her enthusiasm for seeking out new designs and materials, hence the trip to Mexico where she was hoping to be inspired by native designs. She had sent Poppy a hastily scribbled postcard featuring a cat in a poncho and sombrero and had explained that everything was going well and saying that she would be back in a couple of weeks.

As Poppy drove into Walton from York, the city landscapes gave way to fields, still tinged with frost, the tensions of the week started to recede as she listened to the rhythmic swish of the windscreen wipers intermingled with the fruity, deep tones of Amy Winehouse. Friday's strange conversation with Tara Fenton seeped into her mind as she tried to shake off the memory of her screams. Andrea had paled when she relayed everything to her and clasped her hand to her mouth. There had been no news from the police, though Andrea had stayed in the office late to ring round some of her contacts from the local force. She had been unable to find anything out.

'Damn, I tried to contact her when she rang last week, but I couldn't get through. I hope she's OK,' Andrea had explained, her face etched with worry. Then she had smiled. 'Look, you did absolutely the right thing, Poppy. I'm sure it's something and nothing. You go on home and I'll see you on Monday. Have a great weekend and don't worry.' Poppy had the feeling that she was definitely not telling her the whole story, but had reluctantly left the office, feeling troubled and ill at ease, a feeling that hadn't quite gone away. Probably, lunch with her grandparents was just what she needed.

As she rounded the bend into Walton, she nearly followed the road to the Trenthams' yard then hastily turned right into her grandparents' lane, thoughts now turning to Kyle and Tristan. She would visit Kyle next week and catch up them both. Perhaps, Kyle's mood change had been nothing more sinister than girl trouble after all?

'G and T, darling?' asked George as he sat at the table whilst Millicent fussed over the beef. There was the delicious smell of beef, roasted parsnips and Yorkshire puddings. Her grandmother was an excellent cook. Bertie, their spaniel came up wagging his tail furiously. 'I must say it's lovely to see you so soon after the last visit. How are things going with your young charge at the Trenthams?'

'Fine, I think. I've met Jeremy and Laura Trentham and their stable jockey, Tristan Davies. It's a different world but I'm getting my head round it.'

'Perhaps, you've come across Basil Lindley, have you? Smashing chap. Lives up on the hill in Walton Hall. Has a horse there, I think. Sometimes play poker with him, he's rather good, I'm afraid.'

'Yes. I have met him. He seems very friendly with the Trenthams. He's often there anyway.'

'What's that about Basil Lindley, dear?' Millicent laid the table and had a sip of her gin and tonic. 'Now how's my favourite granddaughter?'

Poppy grinned. 'I'm your only granddaughter as you well know. But I'm fine. Grandad was just asking me about Basil and if I'd met him and I have.'

A shadow crossed Millicent's face. 'Yes, it was a terrible shame about him and his wife, Audrey. Audrey was such fun, but they divorced a few years ago.

She went to live with their son in Leeds, I believe. 40 years of marriage wiped out in a blink of the eye.'

'Seems strange after years together to suddenly get divorced,' continued Poppy.

Millicent gave her an old fashioned look. 'Well, I'm sure she had her reasons, dear. He is a mathematics genius before going into business he taught at Oxford apparently. Academic types are not always easy to live with though, dear.'

'Poor Basil,' continued Poppy. No wonder he was always down at the Trenthams. He was probably very lonely.

'Oh, I daresay he's kept fairly busy though. He's involved with the local council and what with his syndicate for his horse, I'm sure he had more than enough to occupy him. Often see folks at his place. Probably a poker game, I shouldn't wonder.' George smiled ruefully. Poppy wondered how much money Basil had stung her grandfather for. He certainly had a high opinion of Basil's gambling skills.

'By the way, has your grandfather told you? We're off to the big race meeting at Cheltenham next week. We're off with the Taverners, you remember them, don't you dear? I'm a bit stuck on what to wear for National Hunt races. We usually go to flat meetings in the summer. But it will be very cold. What do you think?'

Poppy had really no idea but imagined comfort and warmth might be key.

'Smart casual, a warm coat I should think.' She remembered Laura Trentham always wearing her fur headband. 'You can always add a furry hat for a bit of style.'

Millicent nodded. 'I can't wait, what with my success with my treble the other day, I'm keen to have another flutter. So, if you hear of any tips, be sure to pass them on.'

After a splendid lunch, George suggested a walk with Bertie. Just mentioning the word sent Bertie into an absolute frenzy. He fetched his lead and dumped it at her grandfather's feet. They made their way out of the garden and through the footpath at the back of the house. Poppy pulled up her collar and thrust her hands deep into her pockets as they walked. It was a bitterly cold, but clear day. She threw a stick for Bertie who scampered off to find it.

'Here you can see Basil's house, Walton Hall from here. Look.' George pointed to the black and white timbered manor house nestling in the brow of the hill. The house was set high above the valley right on the outskirts of the village and was a restored 16th century manor house. They walked down across the footpath which crossed the private road that led to Walton Hall. Just as they were negotiating the stile that led on to the road, their conversation was interrupted by a silver Land Rover hurtling toward them from the direction of the Hall. Poppy raced forward and pick up Bertie who was busy sniffing something at the edge of the road as it hurtled wildly towards them. She caught a glimpse of the back of a dark head in the driving seat and then a blur of blacked out rear windows. Was it Basil? As he tended to walk to the yard, Poppy had no idea what he drove.

'Bloody idiot,' muttered George. 'He was certainly in a hurry.' Poppy knew she should have made a note at the number plate, as they could easily have run Bertie over. Small chance since she couldn't even remember her own number plate. She patted Bertie. Still there was no harm done, she supposed.

They walked on, enjoying the brief sunshine. The path led them to the far end of the village near the Blooms' cottage.

'Look, that's where the lad I'm looking after is fostered.'

'Ah, the Blooms. Great people. Now he is a wonder in the garden, just look how neat and tidy his place is, George. Perhaps, he could come and tidy ours up a bit?' Millicent was entranced by the large garden with its neat borders. Poppy looked over to where she was pointing, but something else took her eye. There was a silver Land Rover parked outside, with blacked out windows exactly the same as the one that had just sped past them from Walton Hall. Poppy wondered who it belonged to. It looked very expensive. Perhaps, it was the footballer's, Tyler Dalton, but then if it was Basil's car why would he be visiting the Blooms? Still, everyone probably knew each other in such a small village, so it was probably nothing, she decided.

Back at the cottage, Poppy said her goodbyes and hugged both her grandparents.

'Thanks for the lunch. Have a great week.'

'And don't forget to pass on any tips,' Millicent called after her. George rolled his eyes out of sight. 'You know, dear, I think I fancy the life of a professional gambler.' Her grandfather's face was an absolute picture.

## Chapter 12

The yard had a couple of runners at Southwell on Wednesday, so Tristan busied himself with helping school Paddy, aka Earl Grey, a beautiful dapple grey, skilfully ridden by Kyle whilst Graeme rode the other horse, Just A Tick, or Minty, so called for his love of mints.

Jeremy was out on the gallops but intended to catch up with them later. It was very hard, Tristan realised trying to explain exactly how to ride a fence and put it into words. He found he was adjusting imaginary reins and using his legs, but how to get that over verbally was almost impossible. That said, Kyle didn't really need the tuition whereas the same could not be said of Graeme.

Paddy jumped really well, and Kyle rode him beautifully. Tristan made a mental note to speak to Jeremy about Kyle undertaking training at the Northern Racing College in Doncaster. As he watched Kyle navigate the three flights of hurdles effortlessly, he was absolutely sure he had the makings of an excellent jockey.

Graeme and Minty had made another pig's ear of the flight, getting far too close to the second and barely managing to scrape over it. Minty ran out at the third hurdle and decided to attempt to make a run for it back to the yard. Tristan had ridden Minty lots of times and never had any problems with him, once he realised who was boss. It was definitely pilot error, he decided.

'Come on. Turn him round into a circle. He's just playing you up. Quiet but firm, that's the answer.'

Graeme and Minty emerged eventually as the lad managed to get him to circle nicely.

'Keep up that rhythm and canter in a circle.' Graeme looked red faced and his elbows were sticking out all over.

'There's no need to jab him in the mouth. Keep a gentle but firm contact, that's it. Right, when you're ready try the hurdles again from the other direction.'

The chestnut horse and rider managed it this time though they wouldn't win any prizes for style.

'Much better. Right, Kyle you try it and then Minty can go again.'

Jeremy back from going out with the string strode into view.

He paused as he watched both horses navigate the set of hurdles.

'That lad, Kyle, is shaping up pretty well. He seems a bit of a natural,' muttered Jeremy.    'Graeme needs a bit more work, though.'

Tristan nodded, noting that Graeme had been at the yard for nearly a year.

'Yes, I was going to mention him to you for the Racing College. He'd make a good conditional, if he continues to make such good progress.'

'Yes, yes. It's early days, but in a couple of months, maybe...' Jeremy looked at the floor. 'I just wanted to catch you. I've some good news and some bad news.'

Tristan had never seen the guvnor look so uncomfortable. He gave Tristan an apologetic smile.

'The good news is I think we've got some new owners wanting to bring three horses, all well-bred and useful. One is especially good.'

Tristan nodded warily wondering what the hell was coming next. Jeremy examined his feet again and rubbed the back of his head.

'Didn't want you to find out on the day, but couldn't get anyone else and God knows Laura has tried. We've just had his agent on... Clough is booked to ride the two runners on Wednesday.' Jeremy glanced at Tristan nervously. Everyone else has gone to Cheltenham or elsewhere, you see. Anyway, there it is. Couldn't be helped.'

Tristan felt a surge of fury rip through him and struggled to contain it. Breathe, just breathe he repeated, his shoulders stiffening involuntarily. For Clough to profit from his misdemeanours by getting both of Tristan's rides left a very bitter taste in the mouth. The injustice smarted painfully.

Jeremy patted his good arm. 'Knew you'd take it like a man. You'll be back in no time, but in the interim we have runners and no rider. Anyway, good show. I'll see you back at the house.'

As he watched Jeremy's tall, figure stride out of view he made a promise to himself. He would not rest until he found out who had paid Clough to bring him down.


Laura gave Tristan a sympathetic look as she gave Tristan his coffee. Jeremy was on the telephone in the office.

'Sorry about Clough. He really was the only spare jockey that day. I spent ages ringing round and there was no-one, then his agent rang us.'

'No worries.' Tristan managed a smile. 'I'm back at the doctors next week, so hopefully I'll have an idea when I can ride again.' He was amazed he could act so calmly, when all he wanted to do was pummel Clough's smug face in. He couldn't believe the cheek of Clough's agent actually ringing up for the ride. But just channel that anger, Tristan told himself. As an impetuous youth he had had a quick temper, but he quickly realised that playing a long game was a much better option. Reacting hastily and angrily usually didn't resolve things. The key was to focus and channel that energy. Laura was studying him, and he knew she was not entirely convinced by his carefree attitude. She looked rather tired, he noticed and had a distracted air about her.

'Everything alright, Laura?'

She nodded. 'Well, sort of. Jeremy has had a disagreement with Basil, can you believe. It's to do with Pinkie. Jeremy wants to run him in a couple of races before that big race at Taunton in a few weeks, but Basil won't hear of it. Says the other syndicate members are against it too. So, Jeremy has gone along with it, but I hate anything like that. I mean, Jeremy arguing with Basil? It's unheard of. And then there's Madeleine, she has fallen out with her mother about her latest boyfriend and wants to come and live with us for a while. I struggle with her as you know. She has never forgiven me for marrying her father.' Laura blinked back tears.

Madeleine was Jeremy's daughter from his first marriage to the glamorous and brittle Annabel. Tristan had met Annabel briefly and would never have put her and Jeremy together. She was immensely posh and thoroughly spoilt. She had turned up occasionally in her designer clothes and fast cars. Jeremy had already divorced Annabel and met Laura when Tristan came to the yard. Everyone he knew liked and respected Laura who worked tirelessly behind the scenes to make the yard a success. There was the endless hospitality towards the owners, the lads' catering and the generally antisocial hours involved in the sport, which she never complained about. Laura was born into a country family, so knew and loved horses which certainly helped. He couldn't imagine Annabel putting herself out for anyone, but herself of course. He considered Laura far more likeable and much better suited to the role of a trainer's wife. He was surprised about Madeleine though. She must have grown up pretty quickly. The last time he saw her she was about ten, had pigtails and was riding a fat Shetland pony that they still kept in the paddocks here.

'So how old is Madeleine? I can't keep track. She's surely not old enough to have a boyfriend, is she?'

Laura smiled weakly. 'She's fourteen now, so perhaps she is. But the argument was not about Maddie's boyfriend, it was about Annabel's.'

'Ah...' That figures, he thought.

Jeremy wandered back into the room pausing to pat Nelson who sat contently at his master's feet. Jeremy looked flushed and very pleased with himself. He beamed at Laura. Tristan thought he was probably oblivious to Laura's feelings and her obvious unease about the argument with Basil and the impending visit of his fourteen year old daughter.

'Just been on the 'phone to the new owners. They're coming around soon to have a proper look round. Better make sure everything is shipshape and what not. But it's definitely going to happen. They have heard good reviews about us, apparently...'

Tristan was curious to know who 'they' were.

'Great. Who are they, by the way?'

'They're Italian at least the father is, and his two sons are interested in racing and want to get involved too. It's Luca Manfredi and his sons, Nico and Brando.'

The Manfredi contingent swept into the yard in a sleek, black Mercedes with blacked out rear windows. Luca was a swarthy, yet stylish fifty year old. Nico was almost identical to his father but younger, whereas Brando was taller, slimmer and had softly, curling black hair and the looks of a model. Luca was dressed in a black suit and black overcoat whilst the sons wore more casual jeans and hooded tops. They oozed money, confidence and glamour. He could smell expensive aftershave and see the quality of their clothes and the exclusive fabrics. Luca spoke little English interspersed with many Italian words such as 'bene', 'ciao' and 'bella', especially at the sight of Laura who blushed like a schoolgirl. The two sons had probably spent much longer in England and spoke like natives with little trace of an accent. Jeremy ushered them into the house whilst Tristan busied himself deciding to thoroughly clean tack in the tack room. He poured neatsfoot oil onto a cloth and began liberally oiling a bridle with half an eye on the scene that was unfolding before him. There was no trace of the stunning girl he had seen with them at the races or of Niall Devlin for that matter. Tristan knew that the Manfredis would bring money and quality horses to the yard, but he couldn't help but feel a little uneasy. Quite why, he had no idea. There had been nothing of concern noted in his brief research of the family at all, yet he had the strangest feeling that everything had changed irrevocably, and not for the better.

After a short period, Jeremy came around to show them the yard.

'And I'd like you to meet our stable jockey, Tristan Davies. Tristan, these are the new owners I was telling you about, Luca Manfredi and his sons Nico and Brando.'

Tristan shook their outstretched hands and was met by three pairs of brown eyes.

'Pleased to meet you.'

Luca grinned showing white teeth. 'Piacere. Jeremy speak highly of you.' The two sons shook his hands solemnly. Luca spoke to his sons in Italian and they nodded and smiled.

Jeremy led them round the yard and spoke about each horse. They came to Bennie's stable where Kyle had removed his rug and was grooming him thoroughly. Bennie was contentedly eating hay from his hay net. As Jeremy proceeded to outline the horse's progress and breeding, Kyle paled at the sight of the newcomers, pulled up the hood on his jacket and dipped round the back of the horse out of their view. Tristan caught a glimpse of his white face. He looked scared and was clearly trying to blend into the background. But why?

Chapter 13

It was a normal Monday morning and Poppy was chatting with her colleagues and sifting through her emails before going on a visit, when Andrea emerged ashen faced from her office and beckoned Poppy to her. She ran a distracted hand through her immaculate hair and indicated that Poppy sit on a low chair. There was no mistaking her sombre expression as she closed the door.

'Poppy, something awful has happened.' Andrea brushed away tears. 'You know the call you took from Tara Fenton last week? Well, the police have been in touch. A woman meeting Tara's description was found dead in an alleyway in the Bay Tree Estate on Saturday. She appeared to have taken a large overdose of heroin and still had the syringe in her arm.'

Poppy felt the room start to swim.

'The police will be here shortly for a statement from you, but I just wanted to warn you and reassure you that you did absolutely the right thing.'

Poppy sat looking through the window trying to take everything in. She appreciated Andrea tipping her off, but also her comment about her having acted appropriately. Questions swirled around her mind.

'Are they sure it was an overdose? She did sound like she was being threatened to me.'

Andrea nodded. 'Quite. I think that's what the police want to find out. Of course, she was an intravenous drug user, so an overdose in not unlikely, but it is important that you give as accurate account as you can.'

'I'm also sure that she wanted to tell us something about her brother's death...'

Andrea grimaced at this. 'Yes. I blame myself there. I should have tried harder to speak to her after she rang you last time. I gave up after a couple of missed calls which is not good enough. You see I was Tara's social worker a few years back and we got on really well. She was doing fine then, had such promise and now it's all gone.' Andrea wiped her eyes. 'She trusted me, and I feel that I let her down. She was only twenty-three, you know… It's no age...'

Poppy sat contemplating the facts. What an absolute waste of a life. There were so many young people that the care system failed to help. Many ended up in prisons or addicted to alcohol or drugs like Tara. It was so much worse for Andrea having actually known and worked with Tara.

Andrea smoothed down her skirt and composed herself. Poppy felt she had to fill the silence.

'I'm sure that you did everything you could, Andrea. You can't blame yourself. Thank you for telling me. I'll cancel my visit and wait until the police have been in touch.'

Andrea looked up, as her eyes brimmed with tears.

'Thank you, Poppy. It's just whatever we do, however well-intentioned we are, it never seems to be quite enough, does it?'


The police officer was wearing a suit and was young and efficient. He calmly, wrote down everything she told him in spidery handwriting pausing only to clarify certain points.

'Can you initial every page and at the end here, miss, if you wouldn't mind?'

Poppy signed the statement.

'So, what happens now? Will you look into things? I'm pretty sure she knew something about why her brother was killed and there was clearly someone there when she was speaking to me. Supposing they killed her because they didn't want her to tell us what she knew?'

The officer nodded.

'Well, obviously we'll look into it. But as you know the deceased had a significant drug habit, so it could be that she'd overdosed by accident. But we will keep an open mind and look at the evidence.'

Poppy realised that they were unlikely to do anything of the sort. To them, Tara was just another junkie who had pumped herself full of illegal drugs and paid the ultimate price.

Poppy rearranged her visit, tried to complete some paperwork and then disconsolately chased paperclips around her plastic desk tidy. She found it hard to dispel the heavy gloom that had descended upon her. What was it that Tara had said? She had called the other person who was with her when she telephoned 'boss.' Strange terminology and exactly the same words that Sadie has used when she had her 'phone confiscated by the school. Was it just a coincidence? She couldn't tell. It did remind her that she had to go and see Kyle about Louella to see what he might know about the girls' disappearances. She punched the yard's number into her telephone and tried to focus her thoughts.

Kyle appeared even more agitated at the mention of Louella. They were sat in the rest room as the gas heater spluttered into life. It was a bitterly cold afternoon. Poppy pulled her coat around her and was glad she had brought her woolly gloves. Kyle was pacing up and down, his eyes glittering.

'Kyle, I know it's difficult to talk about especially if you were in a relationship with Louella, but we are all very worried about the girls disappearing. It may be something and nothing, but there is a risk that they may be being groomed by older males.'

Kyle looked up at Poppy, his eyes full of anguish.

'All I know is Lou changed, started going on 'bout how her life was gonna change. Said she'd met someone who was gonna' make her a celeb, take pics and that, make her millions.' He raked his hands through his hair.

Poppy nodded encouragingly.

'Were there any clues about who this might be, did she give any names that you can remember? Or any other information that may help us trace them?'

Kyle had his head in his hands thinking hard.

'She said I were too young, she had met a real man now...' he continued bitterly. He appeared to be on the verge of saying more when the door flew open and Mickey hobbled in. He grunted at Poppy and then started to rummage in a cupboard pulling out bottles and lotions.

When he left, frowning at Kyle, Poppy tried to go back over the facts with Kyle, but the mood was broken. Kyle was back in stiff upper lip mode. He reassured her everything was fine, but she couldn't help but compare this restless, jittery lad with the Kyle she had first met. He had purple shadows under his eyes and looked unhappy and ill at ease. Poppy had noticed the frown that Mickey gave him and wondered if there had been further bullying. She said goodbye to Kyle, reiterating that he could ring her at any time and decided to call in at the house.

The yard was pretty deserted and there were several empty stables which suggested the Trenthams had runners that day. There was no sign of Tristan, so she guessed he must have gone with them. She felt disappointed and irritated. Poppy knocked on the door of the house but there was no response.

'Think they're all at Southwell,' came a voice. It was Basil. 'Just popped in to see Pinkie.' He indicated an empty bag of carrots. He appeared to be stuffing something else in his pocket. Poppy caught sight of some binoculars.

'Oh, hi.'

'Is there anything I can help with?' Basil's brown eyes looked full of concern.

'No, no. I was just going to tell the Trenthams I'd called, that was all.'

Basil nodded

'I'll be sure to tell them. Well, you're here again. Can I just say what a splendid job you all do? It must be so difficult. You're damned whatever you action you take in your line of work.'

Poppy nodded, feeling slightly uncomfortable at his praise, but not really knowing why.

'Well, bye then. See you.'

She left feeling ill at ease about not being able to relay her concerns to any other adult who knew about Kyle's circumstances. She decided to ring Tristan later and ask him to keep an eye out for Kyle. His words buzzed round her head, 'she had met a real man, he was going to make her a celebrity and take pictures of her'.

She thought and thought, but it didn't help her identity the man. Many men wanting to impress a girl, could have said that Louella. She was a stunning girl after all. Nothing seemed to make any sense. Her mood low, she made her way back to the office to try and concentrate on her work.

Tristan knew he shouldn't have come to Southwell to see Clough ride, but it was almost as bad to stay away. He composed his face into a neutral expression as Clough smirked at him as he was discussing race tactics with Jeremy. Tristan distanced himself and collared a couple of the jockeys he knew. Swinging their kit bags, about to get changed, he felt a pang of frustration. God, he wished he was riding today. Jake Horton and Charlie Durrant were pleased to see Tristan.

'Now then, mate. When are you coming back? It's really dull without you to wind up.'

'Yeah, should be back anytime, in a few weeks hopefully.'

Charlie gave him a sympathetic look.

'Bad news, bloody Cloughie getting your rides. Bet you're fuming.'

Tristan nodded unsure how much to reveal. 'Listen, you didn't hear anything about the fall did you, no whispers about Cloughie?' Charlie and Jake exchanged a look.

'There's always been a bit of stuff about him taking backhanders, as you know. Thing is I'm surprised he manages to get away with it, the stewards being so hot on that sort of thing. And his riding is often dodgy.' Charlie frowned.

'Yeah, he's a lucky bugger, too. He's had some decent winners on a few horses with very long odds, rank outsiders. Bet the connections were chuffed.'

Tristan nodded, taking this in. He made a mental note to check out his rides and look for any trends.

'So, are any of yours worth a bet, do you reckon?'

Charlie grinned, and they went on to discuss their prospective chances. Tristan wished them well and made his way into the bar where he ran into Graham Kent.

'How are you, old son? Fancy a quick snifter before the race kicks off?' Tristan nodded and was given a double scotch.

'How's that collarbone doing then?'

'Great. I'll be back before you know it.'

Graham nodded. 'Yeah. Not before time, old son, not before time.'

'Meant to ask you Graham, have you heard of someone? He's brought a couple of horses to our place. Just wondered if you've heard anything about him? It seems that Niall Devlin works for him, these days. He's called Luca Manfredi.'

Graham took a sip of Scotch and looked thoughtful.

'I have heard of him, just trying to think...He's rich I know that much, not sure how he's made his money, though. Think he's new to the horse game. I'll ask about.'

'OK. Anything on Melvin Clough at all?'

Graham sniffed. 'Well, we all know he's not quite to be trusted. He's clever though. Doesn't get found out, as far as I can tell. Do you reckon he's in with this Manfredi fella?'

'Could be? See what you can find out and get back to me, yeah?'

Graham nodded. They discussed the afternoon's race card and who was worth backing until it was time for the first face.

'Better give me your mobile number, old son.'

Tristan read it out and Graham, with surprising deftness, punched the number into his blackberry with his stubby fingers.


Tristan hung about, had a brief chat with some other lads and acquaintances. His mood was not improved when Melvin managed a second on Earl Grey, who flew home and was unlucky not to win. Interestingly, he had even been tipped by the local tipster, Milliman. Even Just A Tick, aka as Minty, came a creditable fourth and acquitted himself well.

'Well ridden there,' Jeremy congratulated Melvin who caught sight of Tristan and smirked. Laura put her hand on Tristan's arm and whispered.

'For what it's worth, I can't stand the man either.' She gave an involuntary shudder. Tristan was grateful for her support.

On the way back, Tristan received a text from Poppy. It cheered him up considerably. It would be great to talk to her. He texted back suggesting they meet up later in York to catch up. He felt his mood lift.


*Meet you in The Bluebell at 7.*

# Chapter 14

The Bluebell was situated in Coppergate and was a pleasant, traditional pub steeped in history. Poppy was a little late and found Tristan already nursing a pint. He was dressed in a blue shirt which highlighted his blue eyes, cream trousers and an expensive, grey woollen coat. He looked extremely presentable all told, she realised, her mood lifting. She had barely seen him in anything but jodhpurs, boots and his olive quilted jacket. He grinned at the sight of her and ordered her a drink.

'So, are you OK?'

Tristan frowned. 'Well, I've been better. I hope you've had a more productive day than I have. I've watched bloody Melvin Clough take my rides at Southwell and do a reasonable job into the bargain. Bastard. And I'm still no further on finding out what happened with Bennie.'

Poppy was outraged on his behalf. 'Gosh, that's terrible. How come Clough got the rides then?'

Tristan shrugged. 'Well, in fairness Laura tried to get someone else, but everyone was booked up. And we've got some new, rich owners. Very flashy, they are. Italian or something.'

'Well, that's surely a good thing, isn't it?' The little Poppy knew about racing was that attracting owners was essential. If they were really rich, then so much the better.

'Hmm. There's just something about them. I can't quite put my finger on it… Anyway, how about you? You said you'd seen Kyle. How come?'

Poppy sighed. 'I came when you were all at the races. I had to see him because there are these girls going missing from care. Kyle used to go out with one of them, so we had the bright idea of asking him if he knew where she was going, who she was associating with, that sort of thing. All he knows is that she mentioned meeting an older 'real man' with a car and so on. So, it sort of confirms there is someone in the background. Poor Kyle, he seemed really upset.'

Tristan took a sip of his beer. 'Yeah, the 'real man' comment must have hurt. Ouch.'

Poppy nodded.

'Something is troubling Kyle. It may be this thing with his girlfriend, but I think it's more than that. Do you think still think he may be involved with nobbling Bennie?'

Tristan sighed. 'Well, the obvious person would be Kyle but I don't quite buy it. I have made some general inquiries about Cloughie but I found something interesting out about the horses he's ridden and the odds.'

Poppy was intrigued. 'Great, what exactly?'

'Nearly all of the horses Cloughie has won on had very little form and consequently their odds were long. And one of my bookie friends paid out to Niall Devlin, an ex-jockey with a history of dodgy dealings. He only bet £50 and it was a complex treble or something, hardly worth the bother of nobbling horses for that stake. Unless...' Poppy noticed the gleam in Tristan's eye as he said this. It was as though he had just thought of it. 'Maybe they are building up to something big and it was some sort of trial?'

'Where does Kyle fit in then?' Poppy asked.

'Well, Niall Devlin is an ex jockey who was warned off because of dodgy dealings, he was known to have a bet on the winner.' Poppy still looked confused. 'So, Niall Devlin, Kyle Devlin? Perhaps, they are relatives?'

'So, hang on a minute, are you implying that Niall Devlin is related to Kyle and used that relationship to pressurise him to let Bennie out of his stable, put the glass in the straw, remove the lorry's spare tyre and all that?'

'Well, it's a possibility, isn't it?' Tristan shrugged at Poppy's horrified expression. 'Hey. I'm just thinking it through, not accusing anyone. Do you know the name of Kyle's father? Perhaps, long lost father and son reunite and cement their relationship by organising a betting scam?'

Poppy laughed and shook her head. 'You certainly have a good imagination. Perhaps, you're right but I don't believe it. I don't know the name of Kyle's father, but I can find out. Anyway, why pick on Kyle, it could be anyone.'

Tristan thought for a minute and shook his head. 'Well, that long-lost son thing is just a theory.' Tristan realised that Poppy was quite defensive of Kyle. He admired her loyalty. 'But if I'm honest I don't think he's involved. He seems passionate about the horses and because of that I can't see him doing anything to harm them. Letting Bennie out and putting glass in his stable could have seriously harmed the horse. He's shaping up well as a rider too, so I'd say he has too much to lose.'

Poppy knew exactly what Tristan meant thinking back to her visit when Kyle had showed her round the yard. His excitement and affection for the horses was infectious.

'Quite. It could be Mickey, or one of the other lads? Other regular visitors, other owners, callers to the yard. Someone who comes and goes unnoticed? Does the yard have CCTV, by the way?'

Tristan thought for a minute. 'You know, some of the boxes do. Jeremy usually gives the owners the option of having a stable with CCTV. I think Bennie's owners passed on it, but Paddy definitely does have and he's in the next stable. So, there might be something on that camera. It's worth a look.' Tristan beamed at her. 'Why didn't I think of that? Poppy you're a genius.'

Poppy smiled. 'I wish. If I was I might be able to find out where the girls in care have been disappearing to and find out what happened to Tara Fenton, David Fenton's sister. She was found dead with a syringe in her arm over the weekend. An apparent overdose.'

94

Tristan nodded. 'David Fenton, he was at our place, wasn't he? Shame about him, he was alright. So, the sister is a junkie, is she and she recently overdosed?'

'Yes, except she rang the office wanting to speak to my boss. Something to do with David's death and then I heard someone in the background and she screamed as though she was being attacked. So, I'm not sure it was an overdose. Perhaps, it was just made to look like it...'

Tristan gave a low whistle. 'And you took the call? That's serious stuff. I think we might need some more alcoholic inspiration for this one.'

Tristan listened intently whilst she talked. She found it was great to get things off her chest actually. There were so many frustrating things in her job that they could really get to you if you didn't have support. She used to speak to Jamie and as he worked in a similar field to her, he definitely understood. And Mum. But she was still in Mexico for the time being. Tristan took a sip of his drink.

'Why can't you just follow them from the Children's Home or probably better still track them using their mobiles?'

'Surely, that's illegal and unethical, isn't it? Anyway, I imagine it's complex and the girls would have to agree to their mobiles being used for that, which they are hardly likely to do. The police can trace phone for girls who are missing for longer periods, but these are back within the time frame.'

Tristan shook his head. 'But if you're worried, can't you just do it anyway?'

'No. The girls are on care orders, so it would have to be approved by the local authority and legal team who would not give their consent for that.'

'OK. What do the police think?'

Poppy shrugged. 'In terms of Tara Fenton I very much doubt they will do anything, even though they said they would keep an open mind. To them she's just another junkie who overdosed or took dodgy gear. They can't really help with the girls because we have absolutely nothing to go on. They have come back safe and sound so far, the next day. Maybe a little worse for the wear, but that's it.'

'Well, have you asked them where they go?'

'Of course, but nothing checks out. They were with different friends and don't know their surnames and so on. The information we have got is that Kyle's old girlfriend met an older man who wants to make her a celeb and take some pictures of her. The only information from the other girl is that when her mobile was confiscated in school, she was worried that 'the boss' would be angry. That's it.'

Tristan grinned. 'OK. I am completely stumped. You win, there's nothing to go on at all. Even less than in the Bennie's case. It's hopeless on both counts.'

There was a long pause. Poppy produced her large black diary from her bag and turned to the blank pages at the back. Then she pulled out several different coloured felt tips.

'But we mustn't be defeatist. Let's use a mind map for our ideas and be as creative and as free thinking as we can.'

Tristan looked at the diary, pens and then down at Poppy's bag. 'You appear to have forgotten the kitchen sink.'

She laughed and tore out some blank pieces of A4 from the back of her diary.

'Look, I did a creative thinking skills module at Uni and it has never let me down yet. We start with brainstorming, play with the ideas, think of twenty questions about the problem and 20 different answers for each question, using the mind map techniques. Look you think of something, the keyword, and then add ideas or associations. Like this.' Poppy drew what looked like a word with branches and words radiating off them. 'We each do our problems and then swap over. Are you up for it?'

Tristan grinned. 'What have we got to lose?'

By the end of the evening they had a laugh and had come up with some crazy ideas as well as some feasible ones. Poppy was starting to think that Tristan had a point with the mobile tracking and Tristan didn't feel quite so stuck. He actually had some leads regarding Bennie.

'So, as well as Cloughie, Kyle, Basil is a possible suspect, the frowny odd job man?' Tristan grinned. 'Oh, you mean Surly Gaz and Jeremy and Laura? Are you serious?'

Poppy shrugged. 'Well, I'm just thinking around the subject. Perhaps, the Trenthams are short of money and need to make some pretty quickly. I don't know?'

Tristan frowned. 'But you didn't need to add me, nor Tyler Dalton! Do you mean THE Tyler Dalton! The Manchester City player? Why him?' He pointed at the name.

Poppy laughed. 'Tyler Dalton used to be cared for by the Blooms who foster Kyle, for your information and they still live in the village. They have lots of pictures of him as a boy. He visits them quite regularly, so is around here fairly often.'

'Oh right. I didn't know that. And Basil, of all people?'

'Well, my grandparents who live in the village reckon he's a heavy gambler and he's always at the yard, isn't he?'

'Really? But still...'

She looked at Tristan's A4 sheet and read it out. 'Follow the girls, put apps such as those that you can use to trace your phone if it's stolen, hire a Private Investigator. Get the police to relook at both David and Tara's deaths because if they were murdered it will be by the same person. That's if they were both murdered and it's a big if, then why?' She looked at Tristan. 'I'm impressed.'

'You know it would be a lot easier if we had some contacts in the police. I know, a mate of mine joined up from college but is now a Private Investigator...'

Poppy grimaced. 'Well, I can sort of help on that front. We do work closely with the Public Protection Teams locally and there's always Jamie, but I'm not sure about him really...'

'OK. Who's this Jamie, then?'

'DI Jamie Lynch. My ex. And if I contact him then he'll want our relationship to be back on again, so I won't bother.' Poppy waved her hands as if to dismiss the thought. She found herself flushing. Why had she had to go and mention Jamie of all people?

Tristan grinned. 'Well, we can't have that, can we? My old mate, Matt Bailey, Private Investigator, it is then.'

Chapter 15

Poppy had spent hours researching and devising her group work plan and had located some excellent training materials. The idea was that she and Moira would undertake some safety work with the four girls at The Limes, which included general safety information, but also looked at healthy and unhealthy relationships. Poppy has devised a range of scenarios for the girls to consider, and some YouTube videos she had managed to locate especially for this purpose. The idea was that they could help the girls understand the difference between a caring relationship and a manipulative one. This was going to be harder said than done, especially with vulnerable young people, who tended to see controlling behaviour and violence as evidence that someone cared about them. Poppy had designed several work sessions, but realised that they would need to be flexible, as sessions might well go off track.

As she drove to The Limes, she thought about her evening with Tristan and his take on how to track the runaways. She intended to speak to Andrea about the situation. As the girls were on care orders, the local authority were in effect their parents, so perhaps gaining permission for tracking them wouldn't be too difficult. Then, there was the problem of selling this to the girls as surely, they would need to install an app? They would definitely need the girls' permission in order to do that. Apps were readily available and could be used to locate a mobile if lost, but whatever way she looked at it, she still couldn't get around the consent issue. As soon as the girls realised the implications, they would get rid of the app or jettison their mobile. Neither would be helpful.

She arrived at The Limes and went through the session plan with Moira, the Senior Care Office, who was going to help her.

'So, if we start with the general safety stuff, I've got a quiz for that, so it should generate lots of discussion. The there's a Youtube video to watch about a girl who gets into a relationship which starts off fine, and then ends up with her boyfriend starting to be controlling, isolating her, putting her down, withholding money and then assaulting her. We can ask them to think about how the girl was feeling at different stages and what choices she made and why. At the end we can go back and think about when things changed and what the girl could have done differently. Did you manage to have a look at the video I sent?'

Moira smiled. 'Yes, it's really good. I have explained why you're here and what we're going to look at and they were fine with that. The only thing is that there has been an argument about a lost mobile. Jessica thinks her 'phone may have been stolen at school, so they are all a bit distracted at the moment. We'll see how we go. Lawrence and Melanie are taking the lads to the Leisure Centre for a bit. Thought it might be easier that way, with them out of the way.

'Great. Well, let's get started then.'


As Moira had predicted, the missing mobile seemed to dominate the session. There was Sadie, Louella, Maxine and Jessica. Jessica was fourteen and a rather large girl with a blunt way of speaking.

'I'm well pissed off, Moira. I'm sure that kid at school has nicked it. She were looking at it and asking me what I could do wi' it and now it's gone. Funny innit?' She folded her arms and glowered at Moira and Poppy. 'What do I need protective behaviours work for anyway? I'll just smash their faces in if anyone gives me any crap, won't I?'

Poppy didn't doubt it looking at Jessica's bulk and generally threatening air.

'Well, we can all learn something, Jessica. I know you're really upset about your 'phone, but let's see if we can sort that out later.' Moira's voice was soothing.

Jessica sniffed. Sadie, Louella and Maxine were all fiddling with their phones. Jessica looked longingly at Sadie's. Sadie noticed and moved it out of view.

Poppy took a deep breath. 'Of course, it's very annoying, Jessica. I had a similar problem some time ago, but there is an app you can download, so if your 'phone is stolen or lost, you can trace it easily. It's no hassle and really is easy to use.'

That got their attention. The girls definitely perked up.

Jessica rolled her eyes. 'But if you ain't got a 'phone how can you use it?'

'Good question. But all you need to do is borrow a friend's phone who also had the app and type in your number. You then get a text giving you the exact location of your 'phone.'

Jessica's eyes gleamed. 'What is the app then?'

'It's FindMob and you use it on android or iPhones. That way you'll never be in the situation again.'

Jessica actually looked a little bit sick when she realised how easily she could have tracked her 'phone using the app. Sadie immediately started to search for the app.

'Perhaps, you can ring your service provider and maybe they'll be able to trace yours?' Poppy suggested. Jessica immediately brightened.

'So, if you don't want to be in the same situation as Jessica, then give it a go. But don't take my word for it, try it for yourselves.'

Poppy feigned complete disinterest and watched Sadie downloading the app. The other girls looked like they had already done it. Of course, what she hadn't told them was that anyone with the app could also locate any mobile and hence the whereabouts of its owner.

'Right then, shall we begin?' She began handing out the worksheets and tried to disguise the note of glee in her voice. It had been so damned easy. She could hardly believe her luck.

Tristan moved his arm up and down and turned circles with his right arm.

'Just do that again for me?' Dr Gray's green eyes kept flickering to Tristan's face as he continued to perform the circular movements. It did hurt a bit, but Tristan composed his face to reveal nothing of the discomfort he was feeling.

'Hmm. Any pain at all?'

'No, it just feels a bit stiff, that's all.'

'Any swelling?' The Doctor examined the arm closely.

'Not that I know of.'

'Have you been using ice packs as recommended?'

'Oh yes.' Tristan didn't think it was a good time to mention the comfrey oil he had been liberally applying having raided Mickey's herbal supplies. Mickey swore by the green oil which was contained a natural substance which greatly accelerated healing by promoting cell reproduction, supposedly. Tristan has certainly noticed some good results with the horses.

Dr Gray pushed his rimless glasses back on his nose and began typing into his computer.

'And of course, you have avoided carrying anything and kept your arm immobilised in the sling, have you?'

'Oh yes. I've been really careful.'

Dr Gray raised his eyebrows. 'Well, you would be the first jockey that has. You guys are absolutely mad, if you want my opinion.'

Tristan didn't want his opinion on that, but he desperately wanted to know when he would be back in the saddle.

'So, when can I ride again?'

'I'd say you will be fit in two weeks. The injury has healed remarkably well, so you must have done something right. I'll complete the necessary paperwork.'

'Brilliant, that's just great. Thanks.'

Tristan restrained himself from punching the air. It also meant he had just two weeks to crack on and find out about Cloughie and who had tried to nobble Bennie.

After feeding at the yard, Tristan went back to his cottage, cooked a steak with salad and settled down to think as he ate. He pulled out the two pieces of paper Poppy had given him and went through them. Poppy had written down her list of possible suspects. The exercise he had completed with her, now made him see everyone as implicated in the crime, which in some ways made it harder to focus. Damn. He had forgotten to mention that the yard was being watched by spotters. Then, he had seen them charge off in the silver Land Rover. That had to be significant, surely? He hadn't been able to get the number plate and such Land Rovers were relatively common out here in Yorkshire. He wrote this down. Surely the spotters were implicated in the betting scam? But what betting scam, exactly. Niall Devlin having a small bet on a complicated treble could have just been a coincidence and such a small bet would not have been worth the risk of stopping Bennie from running. Unless they were planning a massive coup and that was just a trial run? He wrote down 'planning a big betting coup but how?' and found he was stuck. What had Poppy said about considering Basil and Jeremy and Laura? What would be their motives? Greed, blackmail, sex, power? These were the main causes of crime, he guessed. But that didn't help either. He didn't think Jeremy or Laura had financial problems and Basil lived in Walton Hall for goodness sake, so it was unlikely he had. Who else might be behind it?

Surly Gaz he dismissed as being not only surly, but not bright enough to mastermind something like this, although he could have been paid to let Bennie out of his stable and put glass in there. He could certainly have removed the spare tyre on the horse box. He put a star next to Gaz's name. Then, he made a

103

list of other regular visitors to the yard and after adding the farrier, vet and corn merchant, he was stuck again. It was no use. He wasn't getting anywhere. Then he remembered the CCTV and made a note to have a root around for the DVDs. He wrote down the dates of the incidents when Bennie was let out of his stable, glass being found in his bedding and the day of the race when the spare tyre went missing, so he would know what dates to look for. He also would find out Surly Gaz's real name and check him out. As a handyman he was often mending fences, gutters as well as maintaining vehicles, lorries and stables, so had access everywhere. No one would be surprised if he turned up in a stable, a field or a vehicle which was a distinct advantage if you were up to no good, he supposed.

He tried to ring his mate Matt, but he didn't pick up his 'phone. He texted suggesting they go for a drink over the weekend. Just as he sent this his own phone beeped indicating that a message had come through. It was from Poppy.

*Are you doing anything on Saturday night? Are you up for finding lost girls? Poppy x*

Tristan had to admit there were probably better ways to spend a Saturday evening. Still, she at least seemed to be making progress, he conceded, which is more than could be said for him.

# Chapter 16

The session had gone better than expected and getting the girls to download the app was a fantastic achievement. They had made good progress with the work and moved on to a video about sexual exploitation. It had also been useful to see Louella and Sadie together. They had studiously ignored each other, except when it came to the part when the girl in the video realised she was being manipulated. Her 'boyfriend' Dwayne, who she initially thought was cool, had a car and was a grown up, had suddenly popped up with a brother and friends who gave her money in exchange for touching her. Dwayne had explained that their relationship was 'special', so 'special', he did not mind her having sex with other boys. In fact, he encouraged it. She enjoyed the attention initially and the drugs and alcohol, but found she was increasingly isolated from her friends and family. She stopped going to school, found the drugs were getting out of control and she was expected to sleep with a whole load of Dwayne's mates. Suddenly the boyfriend who 'understood' her when no one else did, began to force her to have sex with different boys, she was called a 'slag' and the special relationship that she thought she had with Dwayne began to resemble that of a pimp and prostitute. She was hopelessly addicted to the drugs and was having to prostitute herself to obtain them. The whole video was animated and brought the message home in a way that other mediums couldn't.

Sadie had sneaked a look at Louella, as though seeking reassurance. Louella had pushed her breasts together and pouted. Jessica insisted that the girl in the video was a 'stupid slag' and the final message that, 'people who care about you don't make you do stuff you don't want to do' seemed to hit home when Louella stormed off, closely followed by Sadie.

'Well, I think that told us a lot,' Moira had commented, as she watched them leave.

'Didn't it just,' agreed Poppy, even more convinced that her suspicions were not without foundation.


Poppy had not told anyone about the girls downloading the app except for Tristan. She was unsure how it would be received by Andrea and the police. The local authority were so hide bound in procedures and professional ethics, she had no idea how it would be viewed. Probably as interfering and crossing boundaries, she feared. If and when they located the girls, she would consider what to do and who to tell then. For now, all she had done was share with them an app that would help them locate their missing 'phones. She found it hard to concentrate on work. Instead, she pulled out her diary and looked at the mind maps she and Tristan had drawn. What was it that Kyle had told her about Louella? That she had met a real man who was going to make into a celeb and wanted to take pictures of her. Poppy frowned as she thought this through. What did it mean? Were the girls being lured into glamour modelling or child pornography? How would these people convince the girls to strip off? Then, it came to her. By posing as a bona fide modelling agency. That would work. You heard stories all the time about how girls had been 'spotted', so maybe they were being groomed and photographed, the poses becoming increasingly more suggestive.

Poppy googled modelling agencies on her 'phone. There were loads promising fame and fortune, several offering movie parts, auditioning for adverts selling a range of products from fitness equipment to cars and even nail models. Most were no doubt perfectly legitimate businesses. Probably the ones that weren't wouldn't bother to advertise, she reasoned. Once again, she felt completely stuck.

Andrea came in from a meeting looking pale and dressed entirely in black. The reason soon became clear.

'I'm going to go to Tara's funeral this afternoon. I'm not sure how many people will turn up, but I do feel I should pay my respects. I'm dreading it really.' She gave an involuntary shudder. 'First David and now Tara.'

'So, I presume the police have completed their inquiries then, otherwise they wouldn't have released the body?'

Andrea nodded. 'I suppose so. Apparently, there was no doubt that she overdosed, probably by accident. She had fallen in with a bad lot since leaving care and become addicted to heroin and turned to prostitution in order to pay for her habit apparently. It's so sad. She was a lovely, bubbly girl.' Andrea dabbed at her eyes.

Poppy took this in. 'Listen, do you want me to come with you?' The words were out of her mouth before she had time to think.

Andrea patted her hair and shot her a grateful look.

'If you can spare the time, I would really appreciate the company. It's at 2.30. We can travel together.'

Poppy smiled. She had no idea why she had offered to accompany Andrea, after all she had never even met Tara, but it seemed important. Besides, she might learn something useful. It was the sort of thing she had seen time and time again on television. The detectives always went to the funerals and simply observed the proceedings. She had no idea what she might be looking for, but if it worked for them then why not for her?


The Crematorium was cold and serene. There was an overwhelming, slightly sickly smell of lilies. There was barely a handful of mourners. There were so few that Poppy felt pleased she had come along. There was an elderly relative who could have been a great aunt or grandmother, who struggled in from the cold, hobbling badly and leaning on a stick. Her hair was greasy and her face was etched with worries and stress. She was accompanied by a male aged about forty, who was sporting several piercings and wore jogging bottoms and trainers. There were a couple of young women who were better presented. Poppy thought they were probably friends. Andrea greeted a well-dressed, older woman who had taught Tara apparently and that was it. The service was very short, and the minister had hardly any personal information about Tara. He described her as 'popular' and 'bubbly' and merely hinted about the difficult circumstances of her death. Otherwise, he could have been talking about anyone. Andrea sniffed frequently into her handkerchief and seemed genuinely distressed.

'I can't believe how few people are here. There isn't even anyone from the children's home and they knew her really well. Perhaps all the staff have moved on or retired, I suppose. But still...'

Poppy noticed a younger male who came in midway through the service who at least looked smart in a grey suit.

'Bet he's a policeman,' whispered Andrea. She had obviously been watching the same police dramas as Poppy.

Poppy stared at the coffin trying to dispel thoughts of Sadie and Louella ending up in a similar situation. There were a few hymns and the minister summed up with a final prayer. It was a sad and bleak end to a young life with precious little to show for it. As they filed out, Andrea spoke to the elderly lady, who told them that she was a great aunt. Outside in the chilly, November afternoon, Poppy walked past a handful of wreaths and politely read the tributes. One caught her eye. It was a flamboyant wreath fashioned from lilies and ferns with a small black rimmed card attached. It read;

*To Tara. RIP. The Boss x*

Poppy looked round, her blood stilling in her veins. She committed the florist to memory. *Fleurtations.* Perhaps, they would tell who sent them? She remembered Tara's desperate last words. *'No, no, I never, boss.'* Who exactly was 'the boss'? Sadie had used the same phrase when her mobile had been confiscated. Was this just a coincidence? Poppy instinctively looked round, her eyes darting over the mourners. Was one of them 'the boss'? In the driveway, she was just in time to see the back of a dark haired man in dark clothes slide into the back of a waiting sleek, expensive looking car, before being driven away into the grey street. She rushed to the corner of the road to try and catch sight of a number plate as the car sped off, lost her footing and almost fell into the arms of a well dressed man walking in the other direction towards the Crematorium.

There was a polite stand off as they dodged out of each other's way. Damn, the car was well out of view by now. The man's face came into focus.

'My God, Poppy. What on earth are you doing here?'

Poppy blinked, recognition dawning.

'I could ask you the same question.' It was Jamie.


'So how have you been? Why have you not returned my calls?' Jamie smiled at her. His best, disarming smile. His hazel eyes looked full of concern. She had forgotten just how very attractive he was. Even in the café, Jamie had insisted on bringing her to, he was attracting some admiring glances. He was tall, dressed in a stylish grey suit and had a confident and professional air. He sipped his Earl Grey tea and studied her intently.

'I have been absolutely fine, thank you.' Poppy gave him a clipped response, hoping to deflect further questioning.

Jamie gave her a knowing look. 'Come on. Why didn't you return my calls?' He grabbed her hand. 'I missed you...'

Poppy removed it and shook her head. '*You* come on. If you remember, you ended the relationship and then kept coming back. It wasn't fair on me. You can't have your cake and eat it, as you very well know. I think you should have had the decency to stay away.' Poppy smiled in spite of herself. With all the stuff that had been going on and her friendship with Tristan, she hadn't really had time to think about Jamie and his indecision. She had just got on with it and found she was rather enjoying just having to please herself. Jamie's moods were mercurial and unpredictable. She had spent far too long trying to work out what was going on in his head.

Jamie gave her a considering look.

'Well, a guy can make a mistake, you know. And I think that's exactly what I did in letting you go.'

Poppy rolled her eyes at the intensity of her stare and couldn't resist a dig.

'New relationship not worked out how you expected, then?'

Jamie gave her a hurt look.

'Poppy, what new relationship? I don't know what you mean? Because, if that is what you really think, then you're completely wrong.'

Poppy shook her head and sipped her hot chocolate. She was determined not to be seduced by him.

'Can't we be civilised about this?' Jamie sighed.

'Sure, we can. I am simply having a drink and a catch up with an old boyfriend. In fact, whilst you're here I'd like to pick your brains about something. I was hoping to bump into you actually.'

'OK.' Jamie looked pleased.

'It's a professional matter.' Poppy took some satisfaction in watching his face fall. 'There are some girls missing from care and we are really worried about where they are going.'

'Go on...'

'We're trying to work out what is going on. One of them on my case load came back with a new mobile and the other has spoken about meeting a 'real man' with a car. So, we are worried about who they are mixing with. One girl mentioned that she was going to become a celebrity, and someone was going to take some photos of her. Can you ask about and see if any of this rings any alarm bells with any of your colleagues?'

'Well, I can do, but you should really leave police work to the police. And of course, I am not at liberty to disclose information...'

'Well, of course it's strictly off the record. And while you are at it see if you can find anything out about a jockey called Melvin Clough and a wealthy racehorse owner called Luca Manfredi.'

Jamie wrote this in his notebook.

'Well, you have been busy. Who are all these people?'

Poppy told him all the details.

Jamie nodded. 'Doesn't sound like normal social work, racehorses and so on.' Poppy nodded, noticing his smug smile. 'But it means that you will definitely have to see me again, you know, just to hear my findings.'

'I know, I know. But as friends, that's all.'

Jamie looked serious. 'Well, we'll see about that. I meant what I said. I have made a big mistake and whatever it takes I will make it up to you.'

Poppy realised he meant it. The time had passed when she would have been delighted by this statement. Now, she just felt frustrated. What strange creatures men were! It was perfectly fine for him to reject her, but as soon as she rejected him, it was a very different matter altogether. It felt rather good to have the upper hand for once, she had to admit.

# Chapter 17

'So, I've been given the all clear in two weeks. I've just been given some exercises to do and that's it. Brilliant isn't it?'

Jeremy nodded, barely looking up from his entries and Laura smiled, genuinely pleased for him.

'I'm delighted Tristan. You do seem to heal remarkably well. Just as well really given your job. Anyway, there's just enough time to help Madeleine school her eventer Boo. She's coming later on today.'

'Great. It's been ages since I last saw her. What sort of competitions is she doing these days?'

'Think she's doing proper eventing. She wants to compete seriously now. I suppose I'll end up taking her all over the place. Annabel hates horses, as you know.'

'Well, at least you know about eventing, so you can help her.' Laura nodded. 'And I can help out a bit too. But you won't catch me doing dressage. I do draw the line at that.'

Laura laughed. 'Thanks, Tristan. I'm sure she will take advice much better from you, though.  Bacon sandwich?'

Tristan nodded, and Laura padded into the kitchen. She was clearly not relishing the task of helping Madeleine. It can't be easy being a stepmother, Tristan realised. Laura struggled with Madeleine as a little girl, but as a moody adolescent, well it didn't bear thinking about. Perhaps, they would bond over horses? Laura had been a good event rider in her day and knew far more than Tris did about eventing with its challenging three phases of dressage, cross country and show jumping.  And there was precious little help from Jeremy. He was not sure he had even heard any of the conversation, so immersed was he in his laptop.

'Great thanks, Tris. I'm sure you will be a big help to Laura and Madeleine.' Jeremy looked slightly awkward. 'Well, we have some runners at Stratford in a few days. Wanted to enter that Manfredi gelding, Santa Lucia. He's been working really well and is pretty fit. Might have to call in Clough, if that's ok with you? You won't be fit in time, I'm afraid.'

Tristan nodded. He certainly didn't relish the thought, but as he was still out of action, it was all he could do but agree. After all, he couldn't expect the yard to close down completely, but why did it have to be bloody Cloughie? At least it fuelled his anger and kept him motivated to find out what was going on, he reasoned. Think positive and use the anger, he told himself. Then he thought of something else.

'Where did the Manfredis have their horses previously?'

'It was at Joey Gordan's place, I seem to recall. I'm not sure what happened there? It's not likely to be the owners' fault. Luca is a charming fellow. Why?' Jeremy frowned.

Tristan shrugged. 'Just wondered, that's all.'

Joey Gordan was a trainer in the Yorkshire Moors. He had the reputation as a straight talking trainer, who called a spade a shovel. Tristan had ridden a few of his horses and got on well with him. He might be interesting to talk to, Tristan guessed, thinking he might have a very different take on the Manfredis. There was something about them that didn't quite add up. But they couldn't be involved with nobbling Bennie because they arrived afterwards, he told himself. Thinking back to the mind map he had done with Poppy, he thought about the other possible permutations.

'Must be good to have some new, rich owners.'

'Yes, we could certainly do with the money. We're doing alright but could do better.' Jeremy gave him an apologetic smile.

'Who could do better?' Laura came in carrying mugs of tea and bacon sandwiches.

'I was just saying it must be nice to have new, rich owners like the Manfredis. How did Luca make his money?'

'Property apparently. Luca has lots of business interests, I believe.'

Nelson began barking as someone came to the door.

'Oh, it's only Basil.' Laura went to let him in.

'Is everything alright between you and Basil now?'

Jeremy pulled a face. 'Of course, it was just a stupid misunderstanding, that was all.'

'Morning, one and all. How are we all this fine morning?' Basil beamed at them. He was pushing something into his pocket. Tristan could make out the outline of a pair of binoculars.

'Been bird spotting?' Tristan asked.

'Well, there is some splendid wildlife hereabouts.' Basil looked almost embarrassed. 'Thought I saw a red whatsit earlier. Very rare and wonderful. Anyway, how was the string this morning?'

As Jeremy and Basil chatted about the string, Tristan mulled this over. Basil was clearly no bird watcher. Every bird watcher he knew had an encyclopaedic knowledge of the birds' names. Whatever Basil had been doing, he very much doubted it involved watching birds.

After mucking out Tristan remembered about the CCTV. As he had thought, several of the stables had CCTV cameras installed. Owners were usually given the option of using one but often didn't take it. Paddy, the big grey, aka Earl Grey, was stabled next to Bennie and definitely did have one. Paddy whickered at him, clearly expecting some treat and he patted his muzzle as he looked up at the camera. Rather than arousing suspicion by asking Surly Gaz where the monitors and video recorders were housed, he traced the wiring from the camera back into the garage and had a look around. As well as the Trentham's Land Rover, there were loads of tools, bikes, and situated on a table a dusty recorder with no monitor. He explored and found several DVDs in the drawer of the table and checked for any form of labelling. The DVDs were haphazardly labelled in months, so he pocketed a couple that covered the last few weeks or so and left it at that. He figured he could always come back and try some of the others, if he needed to.

The DVDs proved something of a disappointment. Over lunchtime, Tristan pored over them. Grainy and indistinct, they showed Paddy ambling about, calmly chewing hay and Kyle wandering in and out as you'd expect. From where the camera was positioned, it was virtually impossible to see anyone outside the stable and harder still to see people pass the stable in order to get to Bennie's box. He fast forwarded a couple and tried to remember the date when Bennie escaped. It was the same day when Poppy visited for the first time. The 16th November. He studied them again, but it was hopeless. All he could see was Kyle coming in and out of Paddy's stable as he should. Damn. Nothing unusual there. He tipped over the bag and inspected the remaining DVD's. A bill came tumbling out. It was from a garage in York. But again, it was nothing important. It was just for the MOT on the lorry. The account was made out to Mr Gary Hunter. At least he had now found Surly Gaz's name, which he supposed was something.

At evening stables, he found the yard had another new arrival. Madeleine's new event horse was a likely looking bay gelding called Tickety Boo or Boo for short. He found Madeleine dressed in jodhpurs and a sweatshirt grooming him.

115

He hardly recognised her. Tall, with long mid brown hair, a turned-up nose sprinkled with freckles, she was all grown up.

'Now then, stranger. How have you been?'

Madeleine beamed at him. 'Oh, hi Tris, fine, you know.' She screwed up her nose. 'I'm glad to be here at any rate.'

'Things not good at home?'

Madeleine nodded. 'Not at all. Well, you know what mum's like... I'm going to stay here for a bit. I can get to school and believe me, it will be a lot better. It will be great to have Boo on site rather than at livery. Anyway, how do you like my new eventer?'

Tristan ran his hands over the horse's legs and studied his conformation, quietly assessing him.

'How old is he and what's he done?'

'He's five and we bought him from Ireland. He's an Irish Sports Horse, got lots of scope, but a bit green. I'm hoping to take him eventing next year, maybe do a bit of pony club, hunting, hunter trials and dressage before then. He's doing pretty well.'

Tristan nodded. 'Well he's certainly a fine looking animal and Irish too. You can't beat a bit of Irish. Do you need any help in schooling or anything like that? I've a bit of time 'til I can ride again.'

Madeleine beamed. 'Oh yes. I heard about your fall. That would be fantastic, Tris, marvellous.' She grinned just like her ten year old self, only the pigtails had been replaced with a sleek, smooth longer bob and a hint of makeup. But perhaps, underneath it all she wasn't so very different?


Matt still hadn't rung back, so Tristan spent the evening going through the form books and looking at Melvin's rides. There was a sort of a theme about his winners, all having long odds as with Indian Summer, but again when he considered it, the bet that Niall Devlin had hardly been worth nobbling Bennie for. So why had someone tried to do just that? Again, he spent ages on his computer trying to find links between owners and trainers of the respective horses, but if there were any then he was struggling to find them. He pulled out the mind map he had written with Poppy and tried to think things through. Frustrated at finding no link, he googled the Manfredis and then Gary Hunter. Nothing. There was quite a lot on Basil Lindley, however. Surprisingly, he had been to Oxford studied and then taught mathematics. He'd had success with his computer business 'PC4U'. Then the business had got into financial difficulties during the financial crisis and he had been bailed out and taken over by another company, called 'Technico'. Interesting. Basil had then retired. He'd had no idea that Basil had been involved with computers, let alone such a large company. Still, it must have been galling when things started to go wrong for him. He wondered who owned Technico.

He googled Joey Gordan and the familiar toothy grin beamed out at him. His website boasted many winners in the last season, including the handy grey hurdler, Arctic Lion, who was a seasoned and successful campaigner. He googled the name as it sounded vaguely familiar. He searched for images of the horse again and found several photos of Joey in the winner's enclosure, complete with beaming owners. There staring back at him, patting Arctic Lion was Luca Manfredi, flanked by his sons in their shades. He was surprised to find that Arctic Lion hadn't run hardly at all recently. He suspected an injury or maybe the horse had been sold on. He certainly couldn't remember a grey horse being one of the ones that came in the Manfredi string. He googled a bit more and found another horse that had done well with Joey Gordan, Stellina Mia. Again, this was a really useful mare, bay this time, who had won several races a year ago and then had hardly run at all recently. When he googled her, he found that she was owned by the Manfredis, but again he couldn't recall her name being one of the ones that had arrived at Jeremy's yard. Maybe they sold their horses on quite quickly or in the mare's case, she had been retired and now had a new career as a broodmare. Disappointed, he made notes in a book in which he also folded the mind map and made a mental note to approach Joey Gordan for information on the Manfredis. He thought back to the photos on google and then saw a familiar face as the lad for Arctic Lion. Archie Hall. He knew him from years back when he was starting out as a jockey. He wondered if he still drank at the Rising Sun in Market Leighton near Joey's yard? It would definitely be worth a trip out there if so, though he had no idea what he was looking for.

Just then his phone beeped. Great. He had a reply from Matt Bailey. He arranged to meet him, completed his physio exercises and wondered how Poppy was getting on. He would ring tomorrow for a progress report.

Chapter 18

Poppy struggled to concentrate on work, as she tried to plan what they would do on Saturday night if the girls went missing again. She had arranged to meet Tristan and check the whereabouts of the girls and then she supposed they would have a look round and if it seemed dodgy, ring the police. She hadn't thought it through beyond that, but it would be fantastic to find them and bring them back safely. She had no idea what she was rescuing them from really. Perhaps, they were just meeting up with friends and staying out and maybe the disappearances weren't even connected. Sexual exploitation was such a hot topic lately, maybe they had all been brainwashed into thinking all unexplained behaviour related to this. But then she remembered the girls' faces when she had finished her first session about healthy relationships. She hadn't mistaken the looks between Sadie and Louella. It seemed like realisation was dawning for Sadie, at least, and there was something strange about the way they had left the session abruptly. It was almost as though they couldn't quite bear to listen to what was being said. She decided after her visit to another young girl in foster care, she would call in and see Sadie on her way back. After all, if Sadie had started to work things out then she might just want to confide in someone. They had another session planned next week, but if she had read the body language correctly, Sadie might well be wanting to talk, and she wanted to her to have that option.

Before going out on her visit, she briefed Andrea on her session at The Limes, wrote up her notes and thought about Kyle. He spanned the two worlds of the children's home and racing stables. She wondered if he was involved in the betting scam. She really hoped not but decided to investigate the computer system which held the case files electronically. After all, she was still care taking his case for Tina and didn't really know about Kyle or his background. She sat and read through the files for hours, becoming lost in his life and struggles.

Natalie Fell was a sweet looking twelve year old girl, who had just moved into foster care following a dispute with her parents. Her parents had separated three years ago, and this had been very acrimonious. Since then Natalie had moved between her parents, alternately terrorising her mother and then being dumped at her father's. She responded to father's consistency but disliked the boundaries and so instigated an argument, so she could go back to her mother's. This time she was going to behave herself and she promised it would be better, but again the problems would start and her mother would shift her back to her father's. With her mother, Natalie ruled the roost, stayed out late, refused to be grounded when she misbehaved and generally caused havoc. This time, however, her father had refused to have her, culminating in her coming into care. It was a sad scenario of how kids with inconsistent boundaries and options of somewhere else to live, could end up. Natalie was blonde, cute and looked like butter wouldn't melt in her mouth. Her foster carer, Marie Dobson was vastly experienced and not at all taken in by her angelic appearance. She was experienced enough to realise that they were still in the honeymoon period of the placement. Poppy planned to undertake some direct work with Natalie, as a way of getting to know her, and had gone along after school. Marie settled them in the dining room whilst she sorted out the other foster children, dished out snacks, supervised homework and so on. At times like these, being a foster carer made social work look easy, Poppy decided.

Poppy had taken some materials and they both started by doing a collage about themselves before moving on to an eco map. Poppy had taken along her 'box of tricks' which included felts, pencils, some old magazines, glue, scissors and craft materials. It was a well known fact that kids opened up when they were engaged in a task, and whilst concentrating on something else, often revealed more about themselves than they might intend.

'So, let's just use the materials here and create our own collage about us. I'll do one too and then we can chat about them. You can make it into anything that you want. Is that alright?'

Natalie smiled and began rooting through the materials.

'So how are things here?'

Natalie looked at her with the bluest of eyes. 'Fine. I like it so far.'

'OK. Is school going all right, are you managing to get there in time?' Usually, social work teams really tried to keep children in care at the same school. Not only did this minimize disruption, it also meant that a thread of stability could be maintained for the child, even if they had to travel a long way to and from school. As the overall care plan was for Natalie to return back to her mother's care when boundaries were re-established, she had remained at her original school.

'Yeah. It's alright. I have to get up early but other than that, it's fine.'

Poppy studied the pretty blonde with her long hair tied back into a ponytail. She was wearing her grey skirt, thick tights and her bright red school sweatshirt. She looked just like every other schoolgirl, in fact more innocent than most. It was very difficult to square this Natalie with the one described by her mother.

Natalie busied herself covering every inch of her paper with 'Natalies' in distinct curled writing, flowers, boy band One Way Street and pictures of ponies and pink hearts. She also had drawn a picture of her mobile, a smart 'phone very like the one Sadie had been given. Poppy continued with her collage, gluing pictures of expensive perfumes and clothes that she liked the look of, whilst constantly glancing at what Natalie was doing. She had drawn a picture of herself on her 'phone with hearts coming out of it.

'Who are you talking to there? One of your friends?'

Natalie regarded Poppy coolly. 'Not a friend, my boyfriend.'

'Oh great. Where did you meet him?'

'Oh, here and there. He's older and is going to take pictures of me and make me into a celebrity.' Natalie fluffed up her hair, as all traces of the innocent twelve year old rapidly vanished. She pointed at a small dark haired figure on the collage. He had short hair and was speaking on a 'phone and appeared to be under an umbrella of sorts. She had drawn small pink hearts radiating out of the boy's ear. 'I'm going to be the next big thing and earn loads. I just have to play my cards right.'

Poppy's blood ran cold at the similarities to Louella's comments to Kyle.

'And what's this boyfriend called?' Poppy tried to keep her tone as light as possible.

Natalie gave her an old fashioned look, but the shutters had gone down.

'That's for me to know and you to find out.'

Poppy set her face so as not to look shocked. She couldn't agree more.


Sadie composed herself when Poppy saw her.

'How are you Sadie? I thought I'd come around and do some individual work with you before the next group work session. Is that ok?'

Sadie shrugged but looked wary.

'You know we did a collage when I first met you and some other stuff, how about we have another go and a catch up? Shall we start with a life map? We did one before where you draw out your life like a road with the highs and lows being bends in the road. I'll do one too and then we can talk through them. Poppy fished about in her box of tricks and brought out all the glitter, smelly felt tips, magazines and glue. In spite of herself, Sadie had enough of the child still in her to enjoy creative activities.

'Here I'll start mine off.' Poppy drew a bendy road and started to put in significant things in her life, being born, her brother's arrival, parents separating and so on. Sadie took her cue and did likewise.

'So, did you enjoy the session the other day, Sadie?' She raised a pencilled in eyebrow and fluffed up her streaked hair, which was again styled into a bizarre bouffant, fixed with lots of hair spray and clips.

'It was all right, s'pose. Think you're trying to scare us though.' Sadie screwed up her mouth and looked petulant.

'Well, I wouldn't want to do that, Sadie. It's just, I would hate anything bad to happen to you girls, that's all.'

They continued drawing and writing. Poppy had half an eye on Sadie's road map, but also continued with hers.

'The rule is you can put as much or as little of yourself into this, it's up to you.'

'Can I ask you stuff 'bout yours?'

'Of course, what do you want to know?'

Sadie glanced at Poppy's paper and followed the highs and the lows, born, brother born, parents divorced, went to India, got on my social work course, had a great time at uni, met J, split up with J, met T.'

'So, you got a boyfriend, Poppy? Who's this J and T when they're at home?'

Poppy looked at Sadie. She was such a pretty girl underneath all that makeup. She desperately wanted to take it all off and make her the young girl that she was, not this strange child who was trying too hard to grow up.

'Well, J was someone I was going out with. But it didn't work out and I have recently met someone else, T, who is just a friend...'

Sadie gave her a knowing look. 'But you want him to be more, though, do you?'

Poppy thought about this. 'Well, I'm not sure exactly. When does a friend become a boyfriend?'

123

Sadie giggled. 'Yer don't need me to tell you that, do yer?'

'No, but there's more to relationships that just sex, isn't there? It's about wanting to spend time with them, never wanting anything bad to happen to them, putting them before yourself, that sort of thing.'

Sadie looked sceptical and shrugged as she wrote. She had written as a high, 'met B, gave me 'phone, very excited.' She had drawn 'B' in what looked like a field, with a bench behind him and he was under what looked like an umbrella. Perhaps, this was just symptomatic of the awful English summers? It reminded her of Natalie's collage.

'Does B ever come here, or do you meet him in town?' Poppy asked ever so casually.

Sadie shrugged, the shuttered, knowing look reappearing. She put down her pen and started fiddling with her 'phone, her attention wandering.

Poppy realised she wasn't going to get any further information. At least she now had an initial for Sadie's mystery boyfriend, which was something. She wondered if her and Natalie's boyfriend were one and the same person.

Back at the office she rang Natalie Fell's mother to explain about the date for her review, medical and so on. Mrs Fell sounded a lovely, if rather nervous woman.

'Well, she's settled very well for now and Marie is such an experienced foster carer you can rest assured that she's in very good hands.'

'Good, that's great. Let's just hope it doesn't go wrong if she starts disappearing again.'

Poppy took this in. 'Where did she used to go, have you any idea?'

'No, not really. It all started a couple of years ago. She was asked to do some modelling, someone spotted her in the street and gave me a business card.

Course, I refused. A model, I ask you! She's only twelve, but it seemed to turn her head. And then she seemed to go out more, stay out late, come back as though she'd been drinking or worse. She acquired a new mobile, God knows how, said a mate gave it to her and then would dash off as soon as it rang, presumably to meet whoever it was who contacted her.'

'Can you remember the name of the modelling agency?'

There was a long pause. 'I honestly don't know. I'll have a look round and see if I've still got the business card. Funnily enough though, her father never had any problem with her at his. She was subdued there, but then his new wife couldn't hack it, or so he said.'

'So why was she well behaved with her dad?'

'Well, he lives right out in the Yorkshire Moors in the middle of nowhere, that's why. Natalie never got to see her friends or went to any of her clubs. She hated it. I will be able to get her back, won't I?'

'She is accommodated under s20, as you requested she come into care. This means that you can have Natalie back whenever you want. However, perhaps, if you let things stabilise with Marie and see how things progress, otherwise you could be back to square one. Of course, contact can take place whenever, but perhaps let her settle a bit. How does that sound?'

Mrs Fell was sniffing, fighting tears. 'I do love her, you know. I just wish Tony could have helped more, then we wouldn't be in this mess.'

Poppy reassured Mrs Fell, arranged for telephone contact and then face to face contact to take place and then rang off. Whoever, Natalie's boyfriend was, he had clearly struggled making contact with her when she lived in the wilds. Or simply not bothered to keep in contact. Poppy had a terrible sense of foreboding. Was this a coincidence or was Natalie also being targeted by an older man, perhaps even the same man who was involved with the other girls? She couldn't help but feel that Natalie's father would regret his decision.

# Chapter 19

Tristan watched the string and noted that the Manfredi gelding, Santa Lucia, did have an excellent turn of speed as Jeremy had predicted. He was a fine looking bay and had black points and the large, muscular haunches of an excellent jumper. Tristan noted with a pang that not only was Melvin Clough booked to ride him, he also had also been asked to school him at home. It made sense, but it still hurt, especially as Melvin kept giving him a smug grin every now and again when he thought Jeremy wasn't watching. Luca and his two sons Nico and Brando had also come down and were currently watching Melvin soar over the training hurdles with absolute ease. The Manfredis had zoomed into the yard in their sleek, black Mercedes and sort of took over. Shiny and polished, they had the sort of presence and gloss that was very hard to ignore. They also had the habit of slipping into Italian every so often even though the sons, he knew spoke English as well as he did. This was a little disconcerting.

Kyle was schooling Basil's horse Pinkie and Tristan busied himself in speaking to Basil as a way of avoiding Melvin's smirk. Both horses were down to race in a week's time, at Taunton and Jeremy was explaining to them that it was one of the few courses with a steep incline in the last half mile towards the finish line, and therefore tough for jockeys and horses.

Basil seemed dead set on the Taunton outing for In The Pink, and Tristan remembered he hadn't wanted him to run much earlier in the season, although the horse was looking extremely well. As Tristan was still off and Melvin riding Santa Lucia, there was some discussion about who should ride Pinkie.

'Taunton is a splendid course and ideal for all the connections,' Basil explained, 'that's the reason I was holding out for it. He is owned by a syndicate, you see, so I do have to confer with them.'

Jeremy nodded, anxious to avoid an argument. 'Quite. Who do you think should ride Pinkie, Tris ?'

'Well, I think Jake Horton or Charlie Durrant are excellent lads, as you know.' What a pity Jeremy hadn't thought to ask him who should have the stable rides last time, then they might not have ended up with someone like Clough, Tristan thought crossly.

A shadow crossed over Basil's face. 'Yes, yes they are both good. Or how about Marcus Eden? He seems to be in form.'

Jeremy nodded. 'Well, I hadn't thought of him, but if he can make the weight, I don't see why not.' Basil looked relieved. Tristan hadn't had much to do with Marcus, but he seemed to be an up and coming jockey, whereas Jake and Charlie were much more well established to his way of thinking.

'The syndicate chappies are a bit fixed on him, that's the problem. If it was just me, then I would just leave it to you Jeremy, but sadly in this I can't and as they have elected me as their spokesman…'

Tristan was suddenly curious. 'Who are the other members of the syndicate?' He wondered why he had never met them or why they never came to the yard. Still, he supposed it was not that unusual. Trainers didn't usually ask questions as long as the bills were paid. He thought back to what Google had told him about Basil's business problems. Perhaps, he had had to syndicate In the Pink in order to hang on to him? That would explain it.

'Oh, business associates, busy chaps you know. Might not be able to attend the races, but they take a keen interest you know, a very keen interest, I should say.'

Melvin and Kyle both completed another round of fences and eased up to a trot then a walk.

'I think that's enough for today. Walk them off to cool down, will you?'
Jeremy made his way to the Manfredis who were jabbering away in Italian.

'Buona. E'tutto vada per il meglio.' Luca beamed at Jeremy and Basil. Basil
and Tristan exchanged a baffled look. Seemingly his Italian was as non existent
as Tristan and Jeremy's.

Brando translated. 'My father is very pleased. He says it is all going to plan.'
Jeremy smiled back, rubbing his hands together.

'Splendid, splendid.' Anything to keep the owners sweet.


Tristan had arranged to meet Matt Bailey in The Rising Sun at Market
Leighton and he hoped to bump into Archie Hall, his friend from Joey Gordan's
yard, so he could kill two birds with one stone as it were. Tristan arrived early
and ordered a diet coke, deciding that he ought to be more careful about his
weight with his rehabilitation nearly complete and looked round for Archie. The
pub was the yard's local, but to be honest he hadn't kept up with Archie and
wasn't even sure he still worked there. There was a roaring fire and a handful
of customers around but no Archie. He spotted another lithe looking chap with
the give away weathered complexion and small build of a stable lad and decided
to ask about the place.

'You from Gordan's yard? Do you know my old mate Archie Hall, he used to
work there a bit back?'

The blue eyes looked him over appraisingly.

'Yeah, I am from there. Archie left a bit back before my time.' The man's
eyes flickered over Tristan's face. 'Hey, aren't you Tristan Davies from
Trenthams' yard? I'm Jim Day.'

Tristan nodded. 'Pleased to meet you.' Tristan shook the hand he had
proffered. 'How is it going at Joey's? Think we've got some of your old
owners, by the way, name of Manfredi? Italian, they are.'

Jim frowned as he thought. 'No, I don't think I know them. Perhaps, before my time too.'

Tristan grinned. 'I just wondered that's all. They had a couple of good horses with Joey. Think they had Stellina Mia and Arctic Lion, a couple of good hurdlers, if my memory serves me right.'

Jimmy grinned and nodded. 'Oh yes. They are still with us and are a couple of really useful horses. They belong to a syndicate now, I think.'

'Great. Well, at least they're still with you. Who is in the syndicate then?'

'Oh, I can't remember, some business types.' He seemed keen to change the subject for some reason. Are you back riding from your accident, then. I read about it. Damned bad luck so early on in the season.'

'Yeah.' Tristan wasn't sure how much to reveal and decided, as little as possible about his

suspicions regarding Melvin Clough. You could never be sure who was allied to whom. 'Yeah, busted my collarbone and a couple of ribs, but it's all healing and I should be back in a couple of weeks or so. Maybe before that.'

Jim's eyes widened. 'You heal quickly then. It was only four weeks ago, wasn't it at Haydock?' Tristan was distracted as he saw Matt approaching.

'Yeah, it's about that. Look, here's my mate. See you around then.'

Jim nodded as he moved away. 'Good luck with your comeback.'

'Now then Tris, what are you having?'

Matt Bailey was a thick set, tall man who had been a mate of Tristan's from school. They had kept up a little since then, but nowadays didn't mix in the same circles. Matt went into the Metropolitan Police in London and was pensioned out due to an injury he acquired from chasing a stolen vehicle and being involved in a collision. He had smashed an ankle and foot in the accident and was eventually given a full pension. He was left with a permanent limp but missed the drama of the police life so set up as a Private Investigator. Business appeared to be booming judging by the bloom on him.

'Hi there, Matt. You look well. How is it going?'

The two men caught up for a few minutes. Matt had recently got engaged and showed Tristan his fiancée's photo on his mobile. Tristan made impressive noises. Karin was blonde, petite and very attractive.

'Think she's the one,' said Matt soberly. 'Never thought I'd settle down, but this time I definitely will.'

'Well, make sure you invite me to the wedding, won't you?'

Matt grinned and took a sip of his pint. 'Definitely will. It will be great to have a break from work. I had no idea the Private Investigator stuff would take off, but there is no end of work, couples each thinking the other is having an affair, companies wanting staff tailed, even rich parents spying on kids. If ever you get fed up of the racing you can always come into business with me, Tristan. We'd clean up. At least you can actually run.' He motioned to his dodgy leg. All in all, he had coped well with his injury and change in career. He had always wanted to join the police right from being a kid. It must have been a blow, having to give up on his dream job, Tristan decided.

Tristan gave him an update on his life including his latest injury and hopes for the coming season.

'The thing is I am sure my horse was nobbled and think I could be in the midst of a betting scam, then there's this kid in care that works for us who could be involved.'

Matt started to look very serious, his professional instincts coming to the fore.

'Now slow down whilst I take this all in and make a few notes.' He produced a notebook from his jacket pocket. Matt glanced at his empty glass. Tristan took his cue.

'Right I'll just get another round in and tell you all about it.'

Several pints and hours had past when Tristan made his way home. Matt had paid careful attention and assured him he would look into Melvin Clough, Gary Hunter or Surly Gaz and any other suspect Tristan had thought of. As Tristan left, he looked round to say his goodbyes to Jim Day, but saw that he was deeply engrossed in a conversation on his mobile, so just lifted his hand to him. On the drive back, he reflected that it had been a productive evening, when just as he was on the outskirts of Walton, he noticed a car cruise up behind him, its headlights blinding him. Shit, was his first thought, it was bound to be the police. Still he had only had a couple of pints, so he should be alright if breathalysed. He pulled into the side, squinting as the headlights came closer, getting brighter and brighter. He expected a uniformed officer to walk up to him. Feeling vulnerable, he stepped out of the car thinking about how to frame his response. That was his first mistake. Something was very wrong. The car looked to be a sleek black saloon and there were two men in it were definitely not police officers. There were wearing black balaclavas and jackets and were of average height. They had surprise on their side. He was about to ask them what the hell they thought they were doing, when he felt the car door being flung back into his healing ribs, accompanied by the words, 'keep your fucking nose out.' He sank to his knees whilst the other assailant kicked his head with his thick boots. He heard a crack and felt a searing pain. He thought about how much longer he might need to be off after this, and the irony of nearly being back racing again. He felt almost giddy and sick as the two men left him slumped by the side of the road.

'That'll teach yer,' one of the men shouted. Then he passed out.

# Chapter 20

Poppy was watching the news at about eleven, ensconced in her pyjamas and about to retire for bed for the evening when her mobile rang. Seeing Tristan's number flash up she answered straight away.

'Hi Tristan. How are you?' There was a sort of muffled sound and then a faint murmur.

'Sorry, what did you say?'

'I've been beaten up… can you come...'

'Tristan, where the hell are you? What's happened?' Poppy remembered the very last time she had heard something similar when Tara Fenton rang. She was instantly wide awake, ears straining to hear what was being said.

'Where are you? I can't hear.'

She could make out a sigh as he struggled to breathe.

'On the main road into Walton, you know from Market… Leighton… just after the Walton sign...'

'Right. I'm on my way. How bad is it? Do you need an ambulance? No bloody heroics, mind, I'll ring one anyway...'

His voice was more urgent. 'No, no ambulance. No need. Just winded and cuts...'

'OK.' Poppy's mind raced ahead. Who the hell were they and would they come back? 'Just lock yourself in your car and don't get out till I get there.'

Poppy pulled on her jeans and a jumper and threw some antiseptic lotion, painkillers, bandages and surgical tape into her bag from the kitchen cabinet, an LED torch and a large pair of scissors. That, she thought, would do for cutting the bandages and also double as a weapon if she needed it.

Maisy, her housemate, raised an eyebrow at Poppy going out so late. Poppy had already told her a little about Tristan and she merely winked when Poppy said she was meeting him. Poppy didn't have time to explain that it wasn't like that and let herself out into the clear, black night.

Thoughts circled wildly as she waited for the heating in her small Renault to kick in as she drove through the city. She hugged her coat to her and questioned what on earth she was doing going out in the dead of night to meet a man she hardly knew. Yet, he was injured, he had chosen to ring her of all people and therefore it must be important. Something to do with the betting scam, she supposed, otherwise surely, he would have rung one of the Trenthams or someone from the yard? She wondered why he hadn't. Perhaps, he had some more information that implicated them? The night was bitterly cold and the sky clear and star filled as she drove away from the city and into the remote road that led to Walton. Everything looked so peaceful and spectacular at night, she thought, as a fox or cat ran out in front of her, its bright eyes briefly illuminated by her headlights, it's gaze bold and mocking. Once she thought she saw the swoop of an owl and heard its eerie call. It was like another world.

When she arrived in the village, she racked her brains trying to think what way Tristan would have come into Walton and set off on the back road to Market Leighton. She slowed right down, eyes straining through the darkness and spotted his grey Audi by the side of the road. She looked nervously about her, thrust some medical supplies into her pockets and stepped out into the night.

Having driven back to the cottage, Poppy had bathed Tristan's cuts and bruises and tutted over the injuries to his chest and ribs. Tristan had insisted on using ice and seemed to have a freezer full of the ready made packs of varying sizes. She noticed there was very little worth eating in the fridge, inspected the small but quaint cottage and handed Tristan some pain killers.

'So, who did this to you? Who did you say you'd been to see again?'

Tristan looked grey, clearly found it painful to breathe and was manfully trying to hide it. 'I saw my old mate Matt Bailey, you know the ex copper I mentioned. But before that I spoke to someone from another yard, a chap called Jim Day. Think he didn't like my questions, or something. He was on his 'phone when I left, so I think he rang someone. Probably them. Two men stopped me outside Walton. I thought they were the police when they jumped me and told me to keep my nose out. It was a warning.'

Poppy took this in. 'Did you see the car, a number plate or anything?'

Tristan shook his head, slowly. He winced with pain. 'No. They had balaclavas on and seemed to be in a black saloon car or something...'

Poppy frowned as she looked at Tristan's mottled bruised ribs. It felt quite intimate, bathing his bruises and looking at his slim but strong flesh. The bruising would be horrific tomorrow.

'Hope they didn't break your collarbone again, just when it was healing...'

'No, think it's fine.' Tristan started circling his arm in order to illustrate this.

'Well, that's something.' She looked at the split lip and the congealed lump of blood under his nostrils. He looked uncomfortable with her examination.

'It looks worse than it is. Usually does. I meant to say thanks for coming so quickly. I'll be fine now. I'll get someone to help me pick up my car tomorrow. Just give me some more ice packs, my comfrey oil and a bottle of Scotch...'

Poppy shook her head. What was wrong with the man? Was he seriously suggesting she should drive back home and leave him?

'There's no way I'm leaving you unless you let me take you to hospital. Otherwise, let's get you into bed and I'll lock up and kip on the sofa. OK?'

Tristan was surprisingly compliant. In fact, he seemed pleased. She helped him settle into bed, complete with five ice packs.

'Noticed your freezer is full of the bloody things...'

'Yeah, it's an occupational hazard.' He grimaced.

Poppy shook her head. Tristan looked almost embarrassed as she helped him to bed, covered him in his duvet and drew the curtains to his bedroom.

'Thanks for everything. You know...'

She cut him off guessing what he was about to say. Something about how glad he was that she had dropped everything and come to his aid. She felt a rush of tenderness she couldn't quite explain looking into his blue eyes set in his battered face. She found she was struggling to drag her eyes away from his and on impulse kissed him gently on the cheek. Within an instant, Tristan had pulled her into his arms and kissed her passionately, taking her breath away. Abruptly, she pulled away. She tried to disguise her confusion with her brusque manner, but suspected she was not altogether successful. Now was certainly not the time to think about such things. She smoothed her hair and avoided his gaze.

'Try to get some sleep. I'll be just out there. Call me if you need me. OK?'

He nodded an unspoken question in his eyes.

'I'll lock up and keep these by me and we'll talk about it tomorrow.' She fished in her pocket for the scissors. He nodded.

After she had locked and relocked the doors, she scouted around, found some clean blankets and settled down on the sofa. What on earth had they got themselves involved in, she wondered? Was Kyle involved? Her thoughts turned to the weekend when the girls from The Limes and possibly Natalie Fell would give their carers the slip and set off for a rendezvous with an unknown man. It looked like she would be on her own tracking them down. Tristan couldn't possibly be expected to follow them, not given his injuries. And why had she kissed him and then pulled away when he kissed her back? What the hell was she expecting? She was still examining her feelings about him and the meaning of the rush of emotion she felt, when she realised he'd been hurt, the kiss and whether it meant anything or not. She thought it did but couldn't process the information somehow. Exhaustion took over as she drifted off into a deep sleep.

When she woke up, Tristan had left. He must have gone to the yard, she thought, looking at his unmade bed with the duvet cast aside. Idiot, wondering what the Trenthams would make of his injuries and what he would have told them about them. She felt a tremor of unease, enough to make her ring work to explain that she was looking after a friend who had had a car accident. Supposing his attackers had come back? She had booked in visits in the area that afternoon so explained that she would still keep these appointments. Thank goodness, she had had the foresight to bring a toothbrush and a bit of makeup. The makeup she was especially glad of thinking back to last night. No change of clothes, though. She busied herself, had a quick wash and was just poring over her diary and looking at the mind maps thinking about amendments, when he breezed in as though nothing had happened.

'Fancy a bacon sandwich and a cuppa?'

She looked at him in amazement, deciding to mirror his carefree attitude.

'Where have you been, I was concerned about you? Don't tell me you've been into work?' He looked surprisingly chipper for a man who had been beaten up badly less than twelve hours ago. There was some minor swelling to his face, some bruising and he clearly was in a lot less pain judging from his ease of movement.

Tristan grinned and started frying bacon.

'Well, you know what they say, you can't keep a good jockey down. Ice packs and comfrey oil usually do the trick. I've been more badly injured from a normal fall than from those idiots attacking me last night.'

Poppy glanced at the bottle of green coloured comfrey oil that was on the kitchen table. A great deal had been used, she noticed. What the hell was in that stuff she wondered to have caused this transformation?

Tristan placed a large bacon sandwich and a mug of tea down in front of her.

'Sauce?' She shook her head, the smell of bacon making her realise that she was in fact starving. Tristan liberally squirted his sandwich with tomato sauce and started to eat.

'Now,' Tristan inclined his head at her mind maps, 'what does last night's incident tell us, do you think?'

'So, you're not put off, then? I was thinking I could follow the runaways on my own...'

Tristan shook his head. 'And leave you to have all the fun? I find a good beating concentrates the mind. I must have hit a nerve somewhere which means we are finally getting somewhere with the racing scam, at least. Anyway, how do you know where the girls will be?'

Poppy began to tell him about the apps and how the girls had downloaded it unaware that it would lead to their whereabouts.

Tristan paused mid mouthful. His eyes gleamed. 'Wicked.'

Having thought over the facts again and made alterations to the maps in Poppy's diary, they mulled over what the attack on Tristan had told them.

'There must be a connection with the two horses that the Manfredis own or used to own at Joey Gordan's or something else dodgy going on at there that is connected with the incident with Bennie.'

Poppy thought about this. 'But the Manfredis came after the incident with Bennie, so how can they be related? Unless they had an insider? But what about the Trenthams, Mickey, Surly Gaz all the other suspects?'

Poppy pointed to the names on the map. Tristan looked down too running his fingers through his hair. 'Yeah. But something provoked that reaction, there is definitely something they are trying to hide. I have asked my mate Matt to find out about all the others too. Just in case.'

'Great. I bumped into Jamie and asked him to do the same.'

Tristan gave her a curious look, but she didn't have the heart to elaborate.

'It's a long story… So, what did you ask this chap from Joey Gordan's? Something must have freaked him out?'

Tristan nodded. 'It was about two horses, specifically Arctic Lion and Stellina Mia. Both were owned by Luca Manfredi, but he has either sold them or left them with Joey Gordan. Jim Day, the lad I spoke to said they were owned by a syndicate, so presumably sold. I told him that the Manfredis had horses with us now.'

Poppy mulled this over. 'Would that be enough to piss them off? No one would want to lose rich owners? ''

'No. I doubt it.' Tristan frowned. 'The two men told me to keep my nose out, but in more colourful language.'

'Anything else you can remember, their build, accents, clothing, anything?'

'It was dark, they were wearing black, average build, balaclavas. Sounded English, northern type of accent, unremarkable. Smartish black saloon car. Think I'll just have to wait and see what our contacts throw up or take a little trip out to Joey's Yard.'

Poppy's eyes widened in terror. 'What and get another beating?'

'Only if they know we've been.'

Poppy shook her head noticing the 'we' and his assumption that she was going to accompany him.

'Let's sort the runaways out first. I'll just get this.' Poppy's mobile chirruped into life with a message from work. 'Do you want dropping off at your car?'

'Great, if you've got time.'

Tristan followed her out to her car just as Kyle was approaching the cottage presumably to find him. Damn. Poppy having checked her message put the mobile in her pocket. She had been thinking that it might be a little awkward if she bumped into Kyle. He would inevitably draw the wrong conclusion. She wondered how best to play it and decided to smile and brazen things out. Just as she was thinking this, Basil walked from behind the cottage and came into view. Damn. The pathway from his house to the Trenthams went directly past Tristan's cottage. He was obviously on his way there. He politely raised his trilby upon seeing Poppy but his face registered shock at Tristan's bruises.

Tristan was oblivious, his head was down as he tapped his mobile.

'What did you say the app was called again? Findmob? I can't believe you got them to download it. Genius. We'll find those girls in no time.'

Kyle looked from Poppy to Tristan, no doubt taking in Poppy's casual and unexpected presence at the yard.

'Hi Poppy. Thought you weren't coming until next week.' Then realisation dawned. Kyle flushed and looked from one to the other.

Poppy flashed him a bright smile and waved at Basil who was hovering.

'Yes, that's right. I'll see you next week. I'm just dropping Tristan off somewhere.' Poppy opted for the smooth approach but wasn't at all sure it had worked.

'The guvnor wants you when you've got a minute,' Kyle muttered looking at his feet, before heading back to the yard.

Basil looked very concerned. 'My dear boy, what on earth has happened to you?' His hazel eyes were full of anguish.

Tristan shrugged and looked sheepish. 'Oh, just fell over when I'd had a bit too much to drink, that's all.' He clapped his head. 'So stupid. Truth is I am missing riding. The sooner I get back into the saddle, the better.'

Basil looked a little mollified.

'Well, it won't be long now, I daresay. You will just have to be patient. Must dash and give Pinkie his carrots.'

Tristan looked at Poppy as she plunged the car into first gear and swept out of the drive still in a rage. It was mortifying knowing full well what everyone thought. She noticed Tristan's lips twitching.

'You should see your face!'

Poppy swatted his arm and then realised it had probably hurt him. She certainly hoped so.


Having placated some foster carers and set up a meeting to review how Tom Blake's habit of acting out the domestic violence he had witnessed between his birth parents could be addressed. Poppy updated her diary sheets. This time Tom had tied up the foster carers' six year old son which was rather worrying and the foster carers were becoming a little jumpy. Poppy made herself a coffee and caught up on her emails. Again, her thoughts were distracted by Kyle's injuries and the sort of people who had inflicted them and why. What were they getting involved in? She would just have to persuade Tristan to let the police have any information they found out, otherwise God knows what they might do to them. She had to admit she was impressed but also taken aback by Tristan's casual approach and his devil may care attitude. She gave an involuntary shudder. And she had no reason to think that her own mystery might turn out any better if it had already resulted in the murder of two people. David Fenton and his sister Tara. She really must keep in touch with Jamie, just in case, even though she might not want to. Their safety might depend upon it. She must swallow her pride about ringing him. She fished out her mobile and toyed with the idea of phoning him but as her fingers hovered over the keys, decided against it.

Having an hour to kill before she needed to set off on her visit, she did not want to start on her reports or write letters, so she busied herself interrogating the computer database to see if she could find any links between Sadie Jones, Louella Simpson and Natalie Fell.

Natalie had come into care recently, but her mother lived quite close to The Limes where Sadie and Louella were. Mrs Fell had been adamant that Natalie was perfectly behaved when she lived with her father as he lived out in the Yorkshire Moors. What did that tell her? That Natalie either couldn't get to the gang or that they couldn't get to her when she was living in a remote area. She pulled out the collage that Natalie had drawn and studied it. She looked at the picture of Natalie and then her boyfriend speaking to each other on their phones. The dark haired boyfriend was standing in what looked like a park with a swing behind him. He looked like he was holding an umbrella. Was that relevant? Then she pulled out the life map that Sadie had drawn. There was a picture of 'B' who looked similar to Natalie's boyfriend. She had drawn him stood in a field with a bench with an umbrella behind him too. Was this a park? Did they meet up at the local park, she wondered. Certainly, it must be outside. She pulled out her 'phone and googled The Limes area. About ¼ a mile away there was a place called Mulberry Park. She traced her finger on the screen and found Natalie's Street, Castle Road, even closer to the park than where The Limes was situated. Was it possible that they had all hung out at the parks and been targeted by gangs there?

She tapped away again and found that all the girls had at one time or another attended the local High school, North York Academy. Sadie and Natalie still went there but Louella was now in a different school having attended as recently as nine months ago. Was that a link?

She looked in her notes to what Natalie's mother had said about 'her head being turned' when she was spotted in the street by a modelling agency. But then Mrs Fell had had enough good sense not to take her daughter, so she could discount that, she thought. Unless Natalie had approached them herself? Unlikely though, she thought, as she was only 10 at the time. She couldn't possibly have done that without her mother knowing. Round and round her thoughts chased in an endless loop. She had the feeling that she was making absolutely no progress at all. She would just have to wait and see where the girls went tomorrow. She had no idea what to expect.

Back in Walton, Tristan had continued to make light of his injuries and was sticking with his story about falling over when drunk. He had an hour to kill before evening stables, so he booted up his laptop and tried to find out if there were any links between Arctic Lion, Stellina Mia and Bennie. He had felt fine all day, but the painkillers were wearing off now and he felt the dull ache of pain in his ribs. He grabbed then gulped down a couple of tablets, liberally massaged in some comfrey oil and then tried to untangle the knots in his mind.

He googled syndicate memberships. There was some guidance governing how syndicates should be run. They were popular because they allowed the costs of owning and training a racehorse to be shared between many people. He was determined to know who owned Stellina Mia and Arctic Lion, but he would either have to have access to the files or break in to Joey Gordan's office. He googled Joey Gordan and looked on his website but couldn't find out any further information. Joey clearly wasn't an IT man and it appeared that the website hadn't been updated for a long time. He wondered what the syndicate was called that owned In The Pink? He made a mental note to ask Laura as she did Jeremy's books and would certainly know. The various pieces of the jigsaw puzzle chased round his mind. Fleetingly he had an idea, but it disappeared just when he tried to focus on it, like the fragments of a dream that you couldn't recall when awake. Suddenly he felt incredibly tired and achy. Try as he may it was impossible to make any sort of sense out of the swirling pieces of information that kept flitting through his mind.

## Chapter 22

Tristan heard back from Matt the next morning.

'I have some information on the people you wanted checking out. Not much on any of them but I'm still checking up on the Manfredis. Problem is my contact has to go via Europol which takes longer. There is something on Gary Hunter, though. He's got a chequered past, ended up in a Young Offenders' Institute when he was a young 'un. Breaking and entering, TWOC'ing and some offences for violence.'

Tristan found that the hairs on the back of his were standing on end.

'What's TWOC'ing for God's sake?'

'Stealing cars or taking without owner's consent. Quite a bit of form there really.' At last he had something to go on. He went on to tell Matt about what had happened when he had left him that evening in the Rising Sun.

'Shit. So, he was the guy you were talking to when I came in? So, something got to this Jim Day character and presumably it was your questions about the two horses…what were their names by the way?' He could hear Matt scribbling this down.

'Perhaps, it was Jim and Gary that attacked me?' Tristan was thinking aloud.

'Well, he might not be the brains, but he could be the brawn, don't you think?'

Exactly, thought Tristan, his fist involuntarily clenching. What he wouldn't like to do to the prat. They exchanged a few more pleasantries with Matt inviting him round to meet Karin and saying he'd do some more digging. When Tristan rang off, he was still fuming. He took some deep breaths. It was no good rushing in and blowing everything, he needed evidence and the person who was behind the attack on him. Acting impulsively would blow the whole thing. He bit his lip and decided to keep his eyes and ears open at the yard and observe Surly Gaz. He thought back to the voice that had threatened him. He might just be able to identify it.

At the yard, there was the buzz and excitement that could only mean one thing. The Manfredis were paying them a visit. Luca wasn't with them but if anything, this seemed to intensify the presence of the sons. The two men looked so well polished and groomed as though they belonged on a Hollywood red carpet. Intent on finding Surly Gaz, he was therefore irritated when Jeremy's eyes lit up as soon as he saw Tristan.

'Ah, Tristan. I'm just going to get Kyle to school Santa Lucia for Nico and Brando. Or would you like to do the honours since you're nearly back, barring getting drunk and falling over, of course?' Jeremy had been most amused by Tristan's account of his injury and lost no time in recounting this to the two young men. They glanced at Tristan curiously, appraising his injuries. Bloody Jeremy. Tristan flushed and grinned back.

'Well, I did say I was desperate to get back into the saddle and I should be alright to do a bit of schooling.'

Jeremy looked relieved. He clearly wanted to impress the two men and the subtext was that he would rather his stable jockey show the horse's progress rather than an untried stable lad.

Nico beamed and bowed with excessive politeness. 'If it wouldn't be too much trouble for you?' His brother, Brando, doe eyed and probably the most handsome of the two, smiled expectantly.

Tristan nodded. This was too good an opportunity to miss, even if he did feel like he had just gone ten rounds with Tyson, he was damned well going to make the most of it, before Jeremy could change his mind.

Tristan had admired Santa Lucia, the large bay for some time but nothing prepared him for the thrill of riding him. All aches and pains forgotten, he began by warming up, trotting and then cantering before allowing him his head and urging him into a gallop. The gelding had an exciting burst of speed, Tristan found, and he was grinning from ear to ear when he pulled him up.

'Take him over the hurdles then bring him back round again for another circuit, for us will you Tris?' Jeremy looked serious.

By the end of the session, Tristan unclipped his helmet and cooled the gelding off. He was finding it very hard to suppress his excitement.

The two Manfredis looked equally pleased and looked at Tristan expectantly.

'Well?' asked Jeremy.

Tristan nodded. 'He's one of the best horses I've ridden. He has the makings of a very fine hurdler. He'll fill out yet and gain in strength, of course and it also depends on his stamina improving, but I'm thinking top class.'

Jeremy eyed the two brothers and beamed.

'Splendid. My thoughts exactly.'


The atmosphere was even more supercharged when Jeremy insisted on them all coming in for a drink. Laura went pink when the brothers arrived and the effect on Madeleine, who had been quietly completing her homework, was even more devastating. She went pale then bright red and then hid beneath her hair, casting surreptitious glances at Brando with his softly curling back hair and chocolate coloured eyes. He smiled and winked at her causing her to blush further. Poor kid, Tristan found himself thinking. He remembered what he was like as a pimply adolescent and could only sympathise with her gaucheness. Laura was watching proceedings anxiously.

146

'Do you want to go and finish off your homework in the living room?' Madeleine nodded but not before taking another look at Brando before she flounced off.

Laura filled and refilled tea cups from a large teapot and then wandered off to fetch some cake. Entertaining the owners was a large part of the business and Laura worked very hard at this. Tristan gave her a complicit look then helped slice the delicious carrot cake that she came back with. Tristan planned to make his excuses and try and check out Surly Gaz before leaving. It was a Saturday and he knew Gaz would be leaving at about lunchtime. Besides, he was starting to ache and knew he would have to apply ice packs, especially if he was going to be helping Poppy track down her runaways that evening.

'Gorgeous cake,' he took a bite and savoured it.

Laura looked pleased. Jeremy and the brothers were talking about entries for Santa Lucia. He was entered in a race next week, but Jeremy was wondering on today's form whether or not to give that one a miss and go for a better class of race the following week. However, the brothers wouldn't hear of it.

'No. Excuse me, but my father was most particular on that point. He wants Santa Lucia to race on that day at Taunton.' Nico smiled, but it was tinged with steel. 'My father is a very busy man and he has made arrangements to be back for that race meeting. By next week he will be flying to Italy to attend to some family business.'

Brando nodded. 'What Nico says is true. He must run on that day. These are my father's instructions.'

Jeremy looked a little baffled and flustered but conceded the point. There was a touch of menace, particularly in Nico's voice. However, this soon vanished, and the charm offensive returned as soon as Jeremy backed down. Interesting that the race meeting was the same one that Basil had insisted In The Pink race in, thought Tristan. From what he remembered it was an ordinary meeting at

Taunton, nothing special. But he made a mental note that he would check later. He wanted to check which other horses were entered for the race meeting.

Tristan made his excuses and headed out to find Surly Gaz. He was dressed in his mechanic's overalls and was fiddling with the engine on the lorry. Tristan felt his fist involuntarily clenching as he approached him but managed to keep a grip on his temper. Be reasonable and calm, he told himself. Gary may have had a misspent youth, but perhaps he had turned over a new leaf? He was certainly well respected for his knowledge of car engines.

'Now then Gaz. I wanted to pick your brains, if I could?'

Gaz's cropped, balding head popped up from under the bonnet.

'What's happened to you, then?' Gaz grimaced at the sight of Tristan's cuts and grazes.

'Oh, I just fell over after I'd had a skinful last night, that's all.'

Gaz grunted. 'Didn't see you in the Yew, last night. Must have missed yer.'

'No. I went to The Rising Sun, that's why.'

'Don't know it.' Gaz looked unflinchingly at Tristan. 'Anyway, what do yer want to know?'

'Well, I was just thinking of changing my Audi and wondered what you'd recommend, bearing in mind all the travelling we do. It's a bit pricey for servicing, that's the main drawback.'

Several minutes later, Tristan had to concede that Surly Gaz was anything but when asked about his favourite subject, cars. He went through every likely car and had an encyclopaedic knowledge of strengths and weaknesses. Fords were OK and easy to work on, Volkswagen were overrated as were BMW's. Gaz favoured a Mercedes or a Volvo. He mourned the loss of the manufacturer Saab which apparently were no more having continued to make good quality cars and refusing to compromise on quality. This ultimately made them less competitive and contributed to their overall demise.

'It's a pity, a Saab would have suited yer. Mind you can still get a second hand one.  But let me know if you see summat, I'll come with yer or ask me mates at the garage.' Gaz winked. 'Get yer a better deal, see? But if you need any servicing, I'll see yer right. Don't bother with the big garages. Very pricey, they are.'

Tristan thanked him profusely, being acutely aware that he had done him a great disservice.  He was even going to take him up on his offer of servicing his Audi. He believed that Gaz would probably have been in The Yew Tree as that was his local. Clearly, he could have still been contacted and called upon to lay into Tristan in Walton, but somehow, he doubted it. For a start he was a little paunchier than he remembered his assailants to be and from chatting to the other lads, it was common knowledge that Gaz had married a very dominant woman and was rarely allowed out these days. Once off the leash, he was well known for having a few too many.  It was highly unlikely he would have been able to beat an egg, following a night on the tiles, never mind attack him. Tristan could easily check whether or not Gaz was in The Yew Tree and what sort of state he was in.  He made a mental note to do just that. But his instinct was that Gaz was not involved.  More than that, he seemed a genuinely nice guy who had been very badly misjudged. Whoever heard of an attacker carrying out the deed and then offering to service your car? Tristan made his way back to the cottage irritated in the knowledge that he was back to square one.

# Chapter 23

Poppy had been on edge all day. Although, it was the weekend and she was catching up on household tasks, she could only think about tracking the girls later and felt worried and anxious about what might happen. Part of her wanted to forget the whole thing but by the same token she felt utterly frustrated at the lack of progress on the case. They had almost nothing to go on. She pottered about for a bit, vacuumed, slung in some washing and chatted to Maisy and Hannah. They were off into town to some shopping but the thought of going along did not appeal to her. She made her excuses and was considering ringing Jamie when she realised she had missed a message from him with all the drama of attending to Tristan.

She dialled his number. He answered quickly.

'Hi, Poppy.' She could hear the smile in his voice. 'How are you? I could do with meeting up to talk to you about names that you mentioned.'

'Oh. What have you found out?' She could feel her neck prickling with anticipation.

'Bits and bobs. Best speak face to face. Are you free for a coffee about 11am?'

Poppy was immediately suspicious and wondered whether he was using this as an excuse to talk to her about more personal issues. Still there was only one way to find out.

'OK. Where do you want to meet?'

Jamie named a pleasant coffee shop in town. Still with some misgivings, Poppy slung on some makeup and made her way there.

The shop was reasonably full. There were usually lots of tourists in York at any one time and today was no exception. It was a bracing November day, cold and windy. She swept into the shop and found that Jamie was already there. The waitress took their orders, casting admiring looks at Jamie. Poppy had forgotten that this used to happen a lot, as he was a very attractive man. He was wearing his smart, casual clothes and a fitted grey coat with shiny buttons which suited him. He swept his fingers through his hair and smiled at her. He looked rather smug and pleased with himself.

Poppy took a sip of her hot chocolate and after some small talk, thought she would bite the bullet.

'So, have you found anything out about my runaways?'

Jamie smiled. 'Well, yes and no.' He stirred his coffee, glanced about him and lowered his voice.

'My colleagues are pursuing some lines of inquiry but so far we can't find anything to connect the girls or to establish that they are even going missing together.'

'We can't assume that they're not either. Louella and Sadie have been missing at exactly the same time in four separate occasions now. That can't be a coincidence surely?' Jamie nodded but it was clear he wasn't convinced. 'Can't you do more checking, follow them when they go again, track them or something? They might be taken advantage of by God knows who.'

'What makes you say that?' His smile was infuriating.

'Because girls don't usually run off and stay out all night. Sadie is only twelve for goodness sake. Can't you use their 'phones to track them or something?' She certainly wasn't going to tell him that that was exactly what she intended on doing.

Jamie grinned and shook his head. 'Poppy, Poppy. It's not like on the TV, you know. We can't just track people without any good reason, it would be a real breach of their human rights. There are procedures to follow and they have to have gone missing for longer. Especially since I'm told they turn up the next day none the worse for their jaunt.'

'Jaunt? Supposing they are being abused, you'd hardly use that word then?'

Jamie motioned to her to keep her voice down.

'Look. I just think you're getting over involved in this one. Lots of teenagers in care go missing for short periods. Admittedly it's unusual for a twelve year old but we have to look at the facts. Have any of the girls ever made a complaint or an allegation that they have been harmed, for example?'

Poppy thought back to what they had said. When she thought of it like that, no they hadn't actually complained about anything. But perhaps, they were in the early stages of being groomed, so it might not be that clear cut.

'No, but in cases of sexual exploitation they are targeted and groomed so subtly that they don't even know it's happening. They are so vulnerable any bit of attention can lead them off course. One of the girls came back with a brand new mobile, one has spoken about a boy taking pictures of her and making her into a celebrity.' Poppy could see Jamie composing his face into a neutral expression. 'And one mentioned that her boyfriend's name started with a B.' Then she realised how flimsy the information sounded, especially to a tough policeman used to hard facts.

Jamie stretched out his hand towards hers and continued very gently.

'It's not that much to go on though, is it? Many girls are in similar situations. Are you aware of the huge numbers of young lads taking pictures of their girlfriends on mobiles and girls sending indecent images of themselves to boys? I'm not saying it's right, but it happens. Have you actually seen any photos?'

Poppy shook her head. 'But it doesn't mean there aren't any.'

Jamie tried to change the subject. 'Anyway, Melvin Clough is a bit more promising. There have been several inquiries by the Racing Authorities about him being involved in race fixing, or so I'm told by my associates but no actual evidence as such. If he is doing something then it's quite low level, I'd say. Or he's very clever.'

Poppy tried to hide her disappointment. Tristan had already told her that much about Melvin.

'And the Italians?'

'Well, Manfredi is a fairly common name in Italy so I would need a lot more information.' He smiled. 'If they're from Sicily then we might be more concerned.'

'Why? I have no idea whereabouts they come from in Italy.'

Jamie looked her strangely as though he was humouring a small child. 'It's a joke. You know. That's where the Mafia come from. The mob and so on. But I doubt it. So that may take a while longer assuming you can find out more details.'

Poppy couldn't help but feel that she had been brought here under false pretences and made to feel that she was overreacting.

'Now about us...how about going out tonight?'

Poppy shook her head. 'There is no us, I've already told you and I have stuff to do tonight.' Jamie gave her a knowing look. Why did he always manage to make her feel like she was an idiot with an overactive imagination? She'd forgotten the effect he always had to her making her feel that she was not very bright, that her career was alright for a woman, and that she should be delighted to fall in with all his plans and whims at the drop of a hat.

'What stuff? I bet it won't take all evening. Can we still meet up later?'

Poppy finished her chocolate and made her excuses, feeling irritated and annoyed. She had learned precisely nothing and now felt even more ill at ease and restless. Should she call the whole thing off with Tristan? Jamie had made her feel like she was exaggerating and was completely out of line. She would like to discuss this with Tristan, just talk it through with someone who understood. She was just about to ring him when he left her message.

*Shall I come to yours for 7ish? Text me your address.*

She quickly texted him back with the details and found she was looking forward to seeing him.

Tristan turned up on the dot looking smart and fresh in a navy shirt and navy reefer jacket. Poppy offered to make him a sandwich, but he declined and accepted a coffee. Maisy was in the kitchen, so she hastily made introductions. Maisy's eyes swept over Tristan.

'Gosh, you're tall for a jockey, aren't you?' she commented.

'Yeah. I ride over hurdles, so we can be a bit heavier.' He grinned back. Maisy was weighing him up and it was clear she liked what she saw.

'Am I likely to have seen you on the TV?'

'Yeah. I'm quite often interviewed especially if I win.'

Maisy looked rather impressed at this.

'Have you ever ridden in the Grand National?'

Tristan nodded. 'I got a ride last year on Fantastic Mr Fox. Got around and came in seventh. It was brilliant. I had the time of my life.'

Poppy observed proceeding and decided that she needed to call a halt to the conversation, if they wanted to follow the girls. Maisy even looked a bit star struck. She stirred in the coffee, picked up both mugs and headed off to her bedroom, determined to stop them getting sidetracked. Otherwise they were never going to go anywhere tonight. It seemed rather a forward thing to do but they had serious matters to attend to.

'Anyway, Tris and I have things to sort out. Catch you later, Maisy.'

Tristan gave her a quizzical look but followed her.

'Come on,' she hissed. 'We have stuff to do.'

Poppy sat on her bed whilst Tristan was sitting at her dressing table eyeing her rather large makeup collection.

'Sorry about that. I know I seemed a bit rude but I'm anxious about this tracking business.' Poppy kept checking and rechecking her phone.

At half seven, Sadie Jones was clearly where she should be at The Limes according to the map on Poppy's phone.

'Damn, I'll check every half hour or so. Suppose she doesn't run away today? I should have got Louella's number maybe and at least we could have followed her, too.'

Tristan grinned. 'Don't worry. We'll just go another night if nothing happens. Don't panic. Anyway, I heard from Matt my mate, you know, the one who is a Private Investigator. He reckons that Surly Gaz had form and wondered if he was one of the men who attacked me. I was all for thumping him but when I spoke to him, he'd been in The Yew Tree the night before. His story checked out he was as pretty hammered by all accounts. I'm pretty sure he wasn't involved. So, it's back to square one.'

Poppy nodded. 'Same here. Jamie contacted me and made out he had some information. It was just about Melvin Clough though saying that he'd been investigated by the Authorities for race fixing but you already knew that. And I forgot to mention, I did check Kyle's father's name and it's not Niall Devlin, it's somebody Hanley. Apparently, Devlin is his mother's surname and there don't seem to be any ex-jockeys in the family. So, the long lost father or relative theory is out of the question too.'

Tristan nodded and took this in. 'OK. We're no further on at all. I'll tell you what did happen though. I got to school Santa Lucia. The Manfredi brothers turned up, glamorous as ever. That Brando is a right charmer. He had Laura and especially Madeleine blushing. Anyway, Jeremy asked me to saddle him up.' Tristan couldn't suppress the excitement. 'Apart from the fact that he shows real promise, it felt bloody brilliant. I can't wait to ride again. It's less than ten days away now.'

Poppy found that Tristan's enthusiasm was infectious, and she made a mental note to check out Brando Manfredi at some point, this man who was so good looking that even grown women swooned. But she was genuinely pleased for Tristan. There was a brief lull in the conversation. Poppy felt slightly sick with nerves. Tristan inclined his head towards her mobile indicating that she should check it again. Poppy typed in the number again and watched as the map came up, a red mark like an overweight exclamation mark indicating where the mobile and hence Sadie was situated. She checked and double checked the street names as the red mark appeared to float across the map, pulsating as it went. She took a deep breath and showed the screen to Tristan. Sadie was on the move.

# Chapter 24

Having decided for Poppy to drive, they set off into the crisp, cold night to Jamieson Street on the outskirts of the city to where the red cursor was leading them. It blinked rhythmically but remained stationary at that point as they set off, suggesting Sadie had come to a halt. It was now about after nine o'clock and the streets looked fairly quiet, dark and rather depressing.

'I also have an A to Z just in case.' Poppy pointed to the battered copy she kept in the pocket of the passenger street, her senses on high alert. She didn't quite trust satnavs entirely.

'So, what is the plan when we get there?'

'Have a look round then ring the police?' Poppy had struggled with this bit and truth to tell she was rather frightened because of what had happened to Tristan.

'How about **I** go and have a little look, you stay here, and I'll try to identify where they are and anything else, I can find out and then we can ring the police?'

'OK.' Poppy gave him a sidelong glance. As she took in his slim but muscular build, she had to admit that she was very glad he was with her. They drove on in silence to a leafy, well- heeled area on the outskirts of York, not at all what she was expecting.

'Right, how do we know exactly which building it is?'

'I think if we walk towards it, all will become clear. The map sort of enlarges to pinpoint the actual location.' Poppy parked up and concentrated as she studied the handset and playing around with the features. She knew she should have tried this out before now when she was less nervous. Her fingers trembled as she tried to enlarge the picture.

'Damn, I've lost the signal. Let me just try and get it back again.'

Tristan was looking out the car window, getting a feel for the area. It was largely residential, almost genteel and through the dim gloom he noticed that the houses looked large Victorian style semis with three of maybe four floors. The road was tree lined and there were very few people about, a man walking a dog, a couple shrieking with laughter as they tumbled out of a quiet, traditional looking pub situated on the corner. The Black Horse, he noticed. As Poppy cursed and struggled with the app, Tristan continued to scan the scene. He noticed a young lad walking towards them. There was something about his hesitant almost furtive gait that drew his attention. It was almost as though he was checking with something in his hand as he walked. Something about him looked familiar and then he walked under a streetlight and his young handsome face, framed with soft curls was briefly illuminated. Tristan felt a stab or recognition. Bloody hell! What was he doing here?

'Shit it's Kyle. Look over there.'

Poppy looked up. 'What? Are you sure?'

Tristan nodded. 'It was definitely him. He passed under the lamp post and I got a good look at his face. Maybe he's just meeting someone, what's her name Sadie?'

'No, not Sadie. It's Louella he was involved with.'

Tristan was straining to see where he was going.

'Did you get that bloody thing working?'

'Sort of.' Poppy thrust the mobile at him. 'There. It's directing us to that house over there. Bloody hell. It looks quite posh.'

Tristan followed Poppy's gaze.

'OK, let me go and have a quick look. If he is meeting one of the girls, then I'll follow him. Wait here. I won't be long.' With that, Tristan slid out after

Kyle, leaving Poppy open mouthed. What the hell was going on? Why was Kyle there?


Poppy sat there all her senses on red alert. She locked the doors internally, sat on her hands to warm them up, stamped her feet and scoured the darkness for any sign of Tristan or Kyle until her eyes ached. The app was now working perfectly which was bloody typical and there had been no change in the location of the cursor. Sadie was still in the same place but where the hell were Kyle and more importantly Tristan? What the hell was going on? Poppy had no idea and wondered if she should go out and investigate herself. But then she might run the risk of missing Tristan when he came back and being left on her own with God know who or what? As the minutes stretched to half an hour and then nearly an hour, Poppy was in a total quandary. She bit her lip, chewed the skin around her fingernails and tried deep breathing to no avail. He had been gone for well over an hour when she decided that she would ring him. But if she rang him, would that alert whoever was in the house? Or should she go straight to the police and explain what they had planned to do and tell them that Tristan and Kyle had disappeared. She thought of how stupid that would sound, thinking back to her conversation with Jamie. Then she remembered that Tristan had downloaded the FindMob app too, so she could track him. As she pressed the keys on her mobile, she detected a darting movement in the distance and Tristan finally emerged from behind a parked car and came sprinting towards her. There was no sign of Kyle.

Tristan tried the door and mouthed at her to open it before falling heavily in.

'Drive, just drive will you.' He was breathing heavily. 'I think they might have seen me.' Poppy took one look at his face and roared off down the street.

When they were a few miles down the road and Tristan was sure they weren't being followed, Poppy felt it was safe to ask questions. Every so often, Tristan glanced behind them and started to visibly relax and breathe more easily.

'So, what happened?'

'It was a bit strange. The house was on the left there and appeared to be offices. At least there was a sign at the front that suggested they were. I lost Kyle, so I think he must have gone in there.'

'OK. What happened then?'

'I went around the back and had a rummage around trying to see what was going on. There were clearly people there, lights, music and stuff. I climbed on to a wall at the back and had a good look through the windows. There was what looked like photography equipment, those silver umbrella things and young people. I could hardly see because there was only a small gap between one set of curtains.'

What had they stumbled upon, thought Poppy, as she tried to process the information?

'Did you see Kyle or any young girls?'

'Not Kyle but there were a few young girls wandering around. I tried the door or windows but couldn't get in anywhere. Then one of the men saw me and I had to leg it and hide down an alleyway.'

'So, what was going on, would you say?'

There was a pause whilst Tristan thought. 'It looked like a photoshoot and some sort of a party.'

'What sort of photoshoot?'

'I couldn't see exactly but girls were wandering round in very little clothing, there were men about, cameras, you know...'

Poppy felt slightly sick. 'OK. Did you see any of the men or did you get a look at the sign outside the door?'

Tristan turned to look at her. 'I didn't get a clear look at the guys. They looked youngish, that's all. But I did see the sign. It said Boss Modelling Agency. Does the name mean anything to you?'

Poppy nodded. 'Damn I know I have heard of it before but where?' She racked her brains and tried to think.

'So, what now?' asked Tristan.

'I'm just going to make a call.'

Poppy felt oddly perturbed, wired and deflated all at the same time. She needed time to process the information and make sense of it. What exactly was going on? But first she was going to ring the police and give the information anonymously. That way it seemed no questions would be asked about their involvement. She started the car and drove round for a bit, scouring the streets until she noticed a telephone box that looked in a reasonable state. She was back within five minutes, noticeably more relieved.

She answered Tristan's raised eyebrows. 'I didn't want to use my mobile, as calls can be traced. And my bosses would think I'd overstepped the boundaries and it keeps you out of it too. I know, how about we go to the local McDonalds. There is a 24 hour one on the way back. Fancy a Big Mac and a hot chocolate at the drive through?'

'Brilliant. Why not?'

In the confines of the car they ate and talked through what Tristan had seen.

'So, what do you think this all means and what the hell was Kyle doing there? Do you think he is in involved with all this?'

'Got to be, hasn't he? I presume he knew them or how did he get in there?'

Poppy frowned. 'But supposing he was following Louella like we were Sadie? That would explain things.'

Tristan moved his head from side to side. 'Yeah, I suppose...' But he certainly seemed more sceptical.

Poppy took a bite of her burger. 'Do you think it looked like a normal photoshoot, or was it something that could become very dodgy?'

Tristan shrugged. 'Look. I'm not familiar with photoshoots. I ride horses for a living, but it looked like there was a party atmosphere. And you know what can happen at parties? And there was a definite smell of weed.'

Poppy nodded gravely her eye widening. 'Suppose they get the kids there and then soften them up with cannabis, alcohol and then things progress and suddenly there's some sexual stuff going on and the camera is still rolling. Perhaps, that's it. Indecent images obtained under the guise of a legal photo shoot.'

Tristan looked appalled. 'I suppose there would be a market for the photos, would there?'

'Definitely. No question about it.'

Tristan looked slightly sick. 'God, that's disgusting. How old are the girls?'

'Well, two are twelve and one is fifteen. And the law now states that any child under the age of thirteen cannot consent to sexual activity, so it would be rape. If the police can find any evidence. Let's hope they will.'

Tristan shook his head in disgust.

Poppy eyed him. 'Welcome to the murky world of child protection.'

Another thought was troubling her. Best to get it out of the way.

'Right, do you want to kip at mine? I've an airbed.'

Tristan nodded. 'Yeah. If it's alright with you.'

This suited Poppy perfectly as she didn't relish a drive all the way to Walton. Not at half past two in the morning. She felt calmer and pleased that she had telephoned the police. She imagined them raiding the premises and bagging lots of evidence that would put away the gang for a very long time. Something nagged at her brain, though. Kyle. What on earth was he doing there? Was he involved in the gang? Or had he simply followed Louella? He had certainly been distressed enough about her. Then she realised exactly what had happened. He had been there when Tristan had been talking about the app and must have downloaded it hoping to find Louella. He would certainly have Louella's mobile number, so in that case all he had to do was download the app.

'Hey, that's it. Kyle is not involved at all. He was just looking for Louella! He just used the app, like we did.'

There was no response from Tristan and as she glanced at him, she realised why. He was fast asleep.

Chapter 25

So confident was Poppy that everything would be resolved, she was surprised when there was nothing in her emails or messages to suggest that the police had made a grand discovery. She scoured her emails and rang The Limes to find out if Sadie and Louella had gone walkabout over the weekend.

'Yes, they did, the little darlings. But they came back on Sunday a little worse for wear and have gone off to school now,' was the reply from the manager Lawrence Morgan.

'So, do we have any information about where they went?' Poppy asked, expecting that they would have.

'No, nothing. We rang the police and reported them missing as usual, but they came back on Sunday, slept well and have gone into school with no problems. Staff tried to find out where they had gone but again were told the usual rather tall tales. But at least they're back so that's the main thing.'

'So, you didn't hear from the police?' Poppy asked, rather incredulous.

'No. They were going to pop by on Sunday, but the girls were back by then. Sadie came back first, closely followed by Louella.' Poppy took this in.

'Right, I'll call in this week and see how Sadie is doing.'

Poppy made arrangements to visit, her head spinning. What was going on? Surely the police hadn't ignored her telephone call? Perhaps, they were still investigating and couldn't talk about it due to it being an ongoing inquiry? That must be it, she decided. She continued catching up. There was also a message from Natalie Fell's foster carer, Marie Dobson. Perhaps, if Natalie had gone missing then the police had told Marie what had happened when they went around to investigate?

Marie Dobson informed her that yes, Natalie had absconded on Saturday night. She had informed the police who had taken down her details and obtained a description, but Natalie had turned up the next day around twelve noon, tired but unharmed. She had claimed to have met up with a friend in town and stayed the night at her house. She was, however, very evasive about the details of the friend, their full name or address. Exactly like Sadie and Louella. Natalie had gone to school and seemed quite settled otherwise. Poppy was beginning to think she had imagined the whole thing when Andrea asked if she could pop in for a chat. Surely, this must be about the police raid? Something must have happened.

She sat on the edge of her chair in Andrea's room, bristling with expectation.

'It's just about Sadie Jones. I have had DI Bradley on the telephone. Apparently, the police received an anonymous tip off about Sadie and possibly Louella Simpson being involved in some sort of photoshoot which degenerated into a dodgy party.'

'Oh.' Poppy composed her face into a surprised but calm expression.

'It's just to say that it must have been a hoax because when the police arrived there, the building was empty and there was nothing of any concern found in the property, least of all any missing children.'

What? Poppy took in Andrea's sombre and composed expression and realised that she was perfectly serious. A hoax, for goodness sake! The room swam for a little whilst Poppy took a deep breath and tried to compose herself.

'I realise you are very concerned about Sadie, so I just wanted to keep you in the loop, Poppy. But really, as if people haven't got better things to do than actively mislead the police and take them on a wild goose chase. Ridiculous, isn't it?' Andrea pursed her lips into a cross line. 'However, the girls did go missing again, I understand.'

Poppy tried to work out what on earth had happened. She took a deep breath.

'So, has another girl on my case load, Natalie Fell. I've just spoken to her foster carer. She's twelve and went missing on Saturday night and turned up on Sunday around lunch time.'

'Ok, right. Well, it could be related, I suppose.'

Damn. Someone must have tipped them off. Perhaps, Tristan prowling about had alerted them and they got everyone out and removed everything. It must have been a very thorough clean-up operation though. From Tristan's description there would have been a lot of people and equipment to move out. Then she remembered the sign on the building- Boss Modelling Agency.

'Where was building?'

Andrea gave her a quizzical look and consulted her notes. 'It was an office out on Jamieson Street apparently. But there was no-one there and nothing untoward discovered.'

'What was the office used for?'

Again, Andrea consulted her notes. 'It doesn't say but the police will be in touch with the owner of the property and see if it is rented out and who has a key, that sort of thing. I am sure that if there is something to be found than they will find it. He's a splendid officer DI Bradley.' Andrea fluffed up her hair and straightened up her back, coquettishly.

Poppy couldn't help but think that Andrea had rather more faith in the police than she did. Still it was good to see that she was back on form, appreciating men again. Andrea smoothed down her skirt and gave Poppy a determined look.

'Perhaps, I'll just give John, I mean DI Bradley another bell and ask him to look into the owner of the property and inform him that another girl also went missing. Natalie Fell, wasn't it? Who knows, it may prove to be the missing piece of the jigsaw that might help them solve the case.'

Poppy smiled and made her excuses. She was certain that DI Bradley would be hearing quite a lot more from Andrea on the matter. At least she had got her mojo back. Whilst Poppy was left feeling deflated and frustrated. It was abundantly clear that the Saturday night mission had been a complete waste of time. And to add insult to injury, it was viewed as a hoax and a mischievous act of a busy body who hadn't anything better to do! Even more perplexing, when she went back to her desk and sorted through her messages, there were several from Mrs Bloom and the Out of Hours team regarding Kyle Devlin that she had missed earlier. It seems Kyle had gone out on Saturday night and had not yet returned home. Neither had he turned up for work. She texted Tristan and arranged to meet him after she had been to the Blooms. Things were getting out of control and rather scary. But first she needed to speak to Andrea again.

Andrea frowned as Poppy spoke.

'So, yet another young person has gone missing from Saturday? Kyle Devlin? Do you think the disappearances are linked?'

'Well, they could be. Just suppose Kyle followed Louella? He was in a relationship with her previously, remember and was very cut up when she finished things. If you recall I was asked to speak to him to see if he had any information about where Louella might be going, so he knew about the disappearances and had enough about him to see it could be serious.'

'Hmm.' Andrea flexed her fingers and pursed her lips. 'But what I don't get is if the girls are all back and safe and sound then why isn't he? His disappearance could be completely unrelated.'

Poppy took a deep breath. 'But if you consider what he might have been aiming to do which was confront whoever he thought was his rival, he may have threatened to tell someone about the gang. Who knows he could have been set about and left for dead. If the girls are in the early stages of being groomed, then they probably won't say anything, but Kyle could present a real threat to whoever they are.'

Andrea nodded gravely. 'Let me speak to DI Bradley again. In the meantime, if you could go to the Blooms and try and find out what happened just before Kyle went off and check at the Trenthams to see how things were going there. Perhaps, something has happened at work to upset him? We must consider everything. Do you have time to do all this? If not, I'll get someone else to cover your other appointments.'

Poppy nodded, knowing full well that with Tina Barrett still off sick, everyone was as busy as she was.

'No. It's fine. I will prioritise this.'

Andrea smiled. 'Fine, I'll let you get on then.' She was dismissed. 'Can you keep me updated?'


As she drove to Walton, Poppy decided on a short detour to Jamieson Street. She wanted to go to the last known sighting of Sadie and Kyle. Perhaps, in office hours she may be able to talk to whoever ran 'Boss Modelling Agency' and find out a bit more about the business. The street looked completely different in the daylight and it was far busier. She pulled into the nearest car park as she hadn't a hope of pulling into the side of the road like she had on Saturday night, parked up and began walking up the road.

The road still looked tree lined and leafy but a little grimier in the daylight. She looked around and tried to get her bearings. She had parked over by that lamp post the previous evening, which meant the building that Tristan had gone to had to be this one here on the left. She recognised the imposing four storey Victorian semi with the iron railings and large, rather magnificent doorway. As she walked up to it her eyes scanned the building for the office sign that she had vaguely glimpsed, but Tristan had spoken about. She got up close to the building and climbed the stone steps to the doorway. She was sure this was the right building. But there was one very big difference. There was absolutely no trace of the sign Tristan had seen. She fingered the bricks where the sign should be. It felt sticky with a slight residue of something possibly glue, but that was all. There were no drill marks and the brick underneath where the sign should be appeared to be the same colour as the main building. The sign had been glued there by the looks of things and hadn't been there for very long. She looked about her, deciding not to go around the back in broad daylight. She didn't want to arouse suspicion. She retraced her steps to check that this was the right place. It definitely was, she realised. But the door was locked and there was no sign of life. She made a note of the building number, 93, and made her way back to her car puzzling over the facts. As she walked, she noticed something on one of the steps that led to the building. It was a couple of brown pellets. Horse feed or horse nuts to be precise. She had seen them loads of times at the yard and Kyle usually had them in his pockets for the horses. It was a sure sign that someone horsy had been there. Kyle. Perhaps, he had a hole in their pocket? Then she realised that it could be Tristan, except he was wearing his smart reefer jacket that evening, so it was unlikely, whereas Kyle always wore his padded jacket and she was certain he had been wearing it, as usual on Saturday. She drove to Walton her head swirling with thoughts and theories. One thing was clear, it was definitely the right building which meant that whoever had removed the sign and all traces of the photoshoot and party were part of a sleek, polished gang. They must be well organised and highly professional to have swept away any trace of their existence within a few hours. Her heart contracted. This also meant that if Kyle had been captured by such an organisation, he was in real danger.

Then, it came to her. The umbrellas in Sadie and Natalie's drawings. They weren't ordinary umbrellas, they were the silver photographic variety. Both girls had been lured to a photoshoot under the guise of them becoming models. The building had been used solely for that purpose and was made to look authentic with a realistic office sign that had been hastily removed when they realised they were being watched, along with the girls and all other incriminating items.

# Chapter 26

Betty Bloom welcomed Poppy into the cottage. She looked tired and rather wrung out and wasted no time in saying what was on her mind.

'Whatever could have happened to him? I am worried sick about him. He can't have just vanished into thin air.'

'No, no of course not.' Poppy accepted a mug of steaming tea from Betty and produced her large diary and dug around for a biro.

'So, when was the last time you saw Kyle?'

'Like I told the police, he was as right as rain going out on Saturday to meet up with a friend, he said. Usually he's back by eleven. But he never came back.' Mrs Bloom straightened her dress and suppressed a sob. 'At first I thought he'd met a young lady and stayed out or something or got drunk. We tried his mobile but there was no response whatsoever, so now I don't know what to think. And with him not coming back for work, well, he loves those horses. So, I don't mind telling you I'm getting a bit anxious.'

Poppy nodded. She wasn't the only one. 'Did he say where he might be going or who he was meeting up with?'

'No. Me and Mr Bloom, we don't like to pry, you see. You have to respect these kids and their privacy. They will tell you if they want you to know, see?'

Poppy made some notes in her diary. 'What was he wearing, can you recall?'

Mrs Bloom thought for a minute. 'Well, he wasn't dressed up and sometimes he does make a real effort, but he just had his work coat, jeans and sweater, that was all. Where do you think he is?'

'Well, I'm not sure. Did he take anything with him, like an overnight bag, any belongings, a change of clothes that sort of thing?'

Mrs Bloom shook her head. 'No, I've checked, and he just went with the clothes he was stood up in.'

Poppy wrote this down and tried to allay Mrs Bloom's fears, although her own were burgeoning with every minute.

'Sometimes young people do go walkabout but usually they turn up safe and sound. I'm on my way round to see the Trenthams to see if they know anything and I'll let you know as soon as I find out anything.'

Poppy was in deep thought as she drove to the Trenthams' yard. It all pointed to Kyle being abducted. He hadn't taken any belongings which he would have done had he been intending on doing a runner. She felt pleased in a way because it did mean that he wasn't involved with any wrongdoing, but it also meant he could be in much more danger. Then it came to her. Kyle must have downloaded the FindMob app in order to locate Louella, so they could use that to find him. Her heart lurched when she realised that Kyle could have had his mobile removed and, in that case, they were just as likely to find the person who had abducted him. When she thought back to the telephone calls from Tara Fenton and what she had been trying to say about her suspicions about David's death, she felt an icy finger of alarm snake down her back.

At the yard, Laura answered the door. She was led into the kitchen to where Jeremy and Tristan were talking horses. Tristan gave her a rueful smile, whereas Jeremy looked irritable and ill at ease.

'Damned inconvenient and annoying Kyle not turning up. And we have had a visit from the police, what's that all about?' Jeremy's face was flushed. 'Been up to no good, has he?'

Laura gave him a sharp look. 'Poppy, do sit down and have a cup of tea. Where are your manners, Jeremy? Now what can we do to help?'

Poppy gave her a grateful look. 'It is common for the police to become involved quite early on if kids in care go missing. The Local Authority are

Kyle's legal parents, so we are duty bound to take these matters very seriously. I'm sorry you have been let down but for what it's worth I don't think Kyle would have done that if he didn't have to.'

Tristan nodded, his expression sombre.

Laura and Jeremy looked at each other.

'So, you mean you don't think he's just got fed up and decided not to show up. It's more than that?' Jeremy looked worried.

Poppy nodded gravely. 'I think so, yes. And if it's alright with you, would you mind if I have a chat with the staff, they might be able to shed some light on things?' She noticed Jeremy's frown. 'I promise I won't keep anyone very long.'

'Of course, and if there's anything we can do.' Laura looked thoughtful. 'You might want to ask Madeleine. He was reading her dressage test for her when she was riding Boo the other day. Perhaps, he has said something to her? Tristan do you want to go and give Poppy a hand?'

Tristan and Poppy agreed to speak to everyone separately. Mickey grudging admitted that he was a decent kid and they had got along after the earlier hiccups regarding Bennie.

'He's alright. He's been asking about me herbs and that. Seems real interested.'

'Did he seem upset or was there anything bothering him?'

Mickey shook his head. Short, wiry and with the broken nose of a boxer and a similar attitude to boot, it was hard to think of him as someone that Kyle might confide in.

'No. Not that he told me.'

One of the girls, Anna, rolled her eyes.

'Girlfriend trouble, if you ask me. Told me about Louella, was it? Seemed upset 'bout her but more to do with what she was involved in, modelling was it?

I told him to forget her.' She ran her grubby fingers through her hair and continued grooming Pinkie. 'He seemed sort of deep, if you get my meaning, sort of determined. Like he wouldn't rest until he had sorted things. Don't you know nuffin 'bout where he is?'

Poppy sighed. 'Bits and pieces. But not too much. Did he say what he was planning to do about Louella's modelling?'

Anna shook her head. 'Don't think so. I presumed he would talk to her, that sort of thing.'

Poppy thanked her and went to find Madeleine. Tristan had already beaten her to it. Madeleine was cleaning her tack in the groom's room.

'Hi there. I suppose you have heard about Kyle disappearing?'

Madeleine nodded and continued massaging oil into the bridle she was holding.

'Kyle mentioned about Louella and that he was worried about her. He spoke about the modelling but seemed to think it could be dodgy. Do you think he went to find her?'

Poppy and Tristan looked at each other.

'Possibly. Did he say anything else that might help us?'

Madeleine's blue eyes clouded. 'He asked a lot of questions about which horses were running where and whose decision it was where they ran. He also talked about what happened to Bennie a lot. I had the feeling he thought there was something dodgy going on.'

Tristan frowned. 'Like what?'

Madeleine shrugged. 'I'm not sure exactly. He thought it might be to do with betting or something. He said I was lucky to have decent parents and that I shouldn't take them for granted.'

'Do you think he thought you did?' The words were out of Poppy's mouth before she had really thought about it. She couldn't imagine more of a contrast between the rather spoilt and indulged daughter of a racehorse trainer and Kyle, a boy rejected by his family and brought up in care without two ha'pennies to rub together.

Madeleine looked a bit sheepish, seemingly noticing her gaze. 'Suppose he did a bit. I know he didn't get on with his father.' Her frown deepened. 'Do you think he's OK?

Tristan and Poppy exchanged a look. That was something they couldn't answer.

As she was leaving Tristan walked her to her car.

'I have just had a thought,' suggested Poppy. 'If Kyle downloaded the FindMob app then we can locate him or at least his 'phone.'

Tristan nodded thoughtfully. 'Great.' Then a worried look flashed across his face.

'Does your mobile need to be in charge for it to work because, that might be an issue the longer we leave things.'

Poppy again felt alarm pulse through her. Damn, she hadn't thought of that. How long did mobile batteries last? Depending on what you did with them, 12-36 hours? She opened the app and keyed in Kyle's mobile number. She knew you could save locations, so she hastily copied and saved it.

They were interrupted by several more visitors to the yard. The Manfredis in their sleek black Mercedes, accompanied by a couple of jockeys, Melvin Clough and Marcus Eden. Jeremy went to greet them accompanied by Basil who had appeared from nowhere.

'Who are they?'

Tristan's jaw had clenched with dislike. 'Melvin Clough is the weasel faced chap and Marcus Eden in the younger man. He's also a jockey. Jeremy mentioned they were coming to school Pinkie and Santa Lucia. They are both running at Taunton in a couple of days. Both horses haven't run recently but could be in with a shout.'

'No, I actually meant him.' Poppy was staring at beautiful Brando as he chatted to the others. His gorgeous face with its softly curling hair and large, thickly lashed eyes was a real head turner. Nico was also handsome, and the pair looked like film stars that had wandered into the wrong set.

'It's Brando and Nico Manfredi.' He glanced at Poppy and Tristan rolled his eyes. 'Not you, too?'

Poppy looked a little shamefaced. She gave herself a metaphorical pinch and then smiled up at Tristan. She knew how desperate he was to get back into the saddle. To see Melvin Clough constantly benefiting from his absence, due to the injury Clough had caused, must have been very hard to swallow indeed.

'Never mind, Tris. You'll soon be back, don't worry.'

Tristan grinned and seemed keen to press on. She noticed he never dwelt on his misfortunes, just brushed them aside. It made her warm to him.

'Right then. We'll meet up later at mine and see if we can track Kyle down. We'd best get on with it. What was the location?'

Poppy reached for her 'phone and showed him the screen. It didn't mean anything to her.

Tristan peered at the 'phone. Without fiddling with the buttons and magnifying it, it was difficult to be precise, but it looked to be a location about ten or so miles away.

'OK. It looks to be in the Market Leighton area, but we'll double check it later. I'll finish up in an hour. Meet at my place?'

Poppy nodded. She didn't dare articulate what she was thinking. Were they going to find Kyle and what sort of state would he be in?

It was past four in the afternoon and too late to go back to the office so Poppy updated Andrea on everything she had found out.

'Great, I'll pass that on the police. I have discussed your theories with DI Bradley and they are going to step up their efforts to find Kyle and they are taking the anonymous tip off more seriously now. I think they've allocated more officers, so that's good and we are checking with his parents to see if he's had any recent contact.'

'Everyone I've spoken to thinks that Kyle was trying to find Louella and they have mentioned that he was worried about this modelling that she was doing. He thought it was dodgy, so there could well be a link there if you can find out who had access to the building.'

Then she remembered where she had heard of the Boss Modelling agency before or something very like it. It was on a card on the tack room notice aboard, except it read 'ss Modelling Agency', as the corner had been torn off which must have corresponded to the 'Bo' part. It was so bloody obvious! It had been sat incongruously amongst the adverts for grooms and hay as she recalled. And she had copied the exact wording in her diary. She flicked through and found the page.

'Are you still there?' asked Andrea.

'Yeah, yeah I was just looking for something. Try the Boss Modelling Agency.' She read out the details, realisation flooding over her. How had she missed that? There was even a twitter address on the card, @boss models. Then she remembered Tara Fenton's funeral and the wreath from The Boss. What did it all mean? She felt a chill down her spine. It meant that the deaths of David and Tara Fenton, the disappearance of the girls and the racing scam were all linked. Without a doubt. All she had to do was to find out how.

# Chapter 27

Rather than driving back to the office Poppy decided to call in at her grandparents. Her nerves were frazzled, and it would be nice to see a friendly face. As usual, they were delighted to see her.

'Cup of tea, sweetheart? Piece of cake?' asked Millicent.

Poppy fussed their spaniel Bertie and sat with her grandfather.

'So, I bet you've been at the Trenthams again, have you? How are things there? Do you have any tips for us?'

Millicent came in struggling with a huge tea tray. Poppy found that it was really hard to come up with a neutral topic of conversation. She had so much in her head that she couldn't tell them. She racked her brains. Maybe she could help with tips, though. She thought back to the runners that Tristan had mentioned.

'I do know they have Santa Lucia and In The Pink running at Taunton on Saturday. They could run well, or so I hear.'

Millicent's blue eyes sparkled with excitement. 'Strange that you should say that because we bumped into Basil Lindley the other day. He seemed to have a big party or something going on at the Hall, so he was busy, but he gave me some tips.'

George rolled his eyes as Millicent fished a list out of her pocket. She ignored her husband.

'It's for a Yankee. I just asked him outright for any pointers and he said to keep it hush hush. But there's no harm telling Poppy, is there George?'

Poppy was completely bemused. 'What on earth is a Yankee, I've never even heard of it?'

George sniffed, disapprovingly. 'Oh, it's one of those complicated bets where you choose four horses and place bets on a combination of doubles and trebles. It's really tricky. I don't know why you can't just have a straightforward each way bet, like everyone else.'

Millicent beamed. 'Because that is absolutely no fun. Look, your grandfather didn't explain it well at all. You pick four horses racing anywhere on a particular day and back them to win in every combination of doubles and trebles and then have a final four fold bet on all four to win. So, there's eleven bets in total. The bookies pay out if you have two or more winners. It's just much more thrilling. I think anyway.'

Poppy was completely lost. Millicent found the piece of paper.

'But Santa Lucia and In The Pink's names are on there, look. I'm definitely going to have a punt on that lot. Especially with you and Basil mentioning them. You should too. Look, I'll write the other horses down for you.'

Poppy took a sip of her tea. Her grandmother's recent interest in betting was quite baffling, but she was interested in the information about Basil.

'So, does Basil Lindley have a lot of parties?' She didn't have him down as a partying type, but what did she know? She only ever saw the polite, aristocratic persona he chose to present.

George frowned. 'Oh, probably full of intellectual types. He was a maths lecturer and they probably talk about God knows what. Mathematical equations, I shouldn't wonder and so on. Mind you, you'd need have a maths degree to understand this betting malarkey, especially those Yankee thingies.'

Poppy had a vague realisation that she was not the best company at the moment and sipped her tea whilst the conversation floundered.

'We had another card from your mum this morning. She will be back soon,' continued Millicent.

'It's in about a couple of weeks, isn't it?' asked George.

'Yes, just in time for the Christmas rush, no doubt, what with it being nearly December. But it will be great to have her back again, won't it, Poppy?'

Poppy nodded. She suddenly felt an overwhelming need to talk to her mother and her mood plummeted even further. She would understand about Kyle, Jamie and all that stuff. And she would be able to advise her on what to do. Mum was energetic, sensible and full of common sense. Poppy looked at her grandparents and decided that she couldn't burden them with any of this. They were old and were likely to worry, and she would hate to cause them any concern. Instead, she plastered a smile on her face. But her heart just wasn't in it. As she said her goodbyes, her grandmother pressed the piece of paper into her hand.

'Here you are, dear. Why don't you have a little flutter? It might just cheer you up.'

George gave a wry look as he hugged her. 'See you soon, sweetheart. And I hope whatever's on your mind is sorted out soon.'

Poppy smiled back at them with real affection. So much for trying to hide what she was feeling. Who did she think she was fooling? Not them that was for sure.

She bought drinks and some chocolate bars from the local shop and made her way to Tristan's cottage. Tristan showed her in as he was making preparations for their mission. He dug out a scarf, gloves and black woolly hat, searched his padded jacket for his penknife, found a small torch, ball of bright orange bailer twine and matches. He added some blankets for good measure. Poppy eyed the penknife dubiously.

'Oh, I always carry this around for cutting baler twine, making quick repairs and,' he picked at it, and pulled out a small hoof pick. 'Look. Perfect to remove a stone from a horse's hoof. Don't worry, I'm not intending on stabbing anyone.'

Poppy nodded. Tristan swept up his 'phone and keys. 'Right. Do you want to check the app again?'

Poppy pulled out her 'phone and with shaking hands typed in Kyle's number and waited for a signal. Apprehension flooded over her, but they needed to get there as soon as possible. Kyle's safety and even his life might well depend on it.

'OK, let's go.'


They followed the cursor blinking on the screen to somewhere just outside Market Leighton. It was getting dark as they drove on down a thin track which was getting progressively more and more remote.

'Do you think this is right?' Poppy asked as Tristan peered at the mobile's screen.

'I think so. It stands to reason whoever's has got him would keep him somewhere quite out of the way, don't you think? Just drive on for a bit and let's see where we end up.'

Poppy took a deep breath, continued to drive over a slight incline, scanning the growing darkness as she went. The scrunch of the stones on the road was almost deafening.

'Right, we're getting closer, we're almost here,' muttered Tristan, eyes glued to the mobile's screen.

The track was becoming increasingly bumpy and poorly maintained.

'Look. Over there.' Poppy pointed to a grey outline to the left of them that was briefly illuminated by her headlights. It was an old stone barn by the look of it. As they were heading down the track Poppy killed her headlights and engine.

'What did you do that for?' hissed Tristan.

'We don't want to alert anyone...'

'Yes, but now we can't see. Just put your sidelights on.'

Poppy flicked a switch and came to a halt at the side of the track.

Tristan searched in his pockets dug out his torch and pulled down his woolly hat.

'Right. I'll go and have a quick look. You stay here and be ready to drive at a moment's notice.'

'Wait, can we use a signal to communicate with each other?' Poppy didn't want to be left anxious and with no means of communication like she was the previous evening.

Tristan thought for a bit. 'If you have another torch we could flash once for all clear, all OK and twice for danger, get out of here.'

Poppy rummaged around in her glove box and triumphantly produced her small, yet bright LED torch. Her white face was briefly illuminated as she tried it.

'OK, at least it works. Don't forget one flash for all clear and twice for danger. OK?'

Poppy nodded and took a deep breath.

Tristan opened the car door, climbed out and set off across the field, his jaw set in grim determination.


The barn was poorly maintained at one end with a large gaping hole where roof tiles had fallen in, showing the inky black sky above. At the other side there was a small stable which looked as though it had a hayloft over it. There were signs of recent use. The floor had straw swept to one side and had some farm implements and old tools neatly stacked in one corner. Tristan shone his torch round the roof which was boarded out but looked basically sound and intact. He listened, his ears straining for any sort of noise and shone the torch around searching every inch of the ancient, grey stonework. It was then that he heard a faint, muffled mewing sound that could have been from a human or wild animal. The mewing continued and seemed to be coming from the hayloft above. He went to the rear of the barn and found a series of old stone steps and carefully climbed up steadily one by one. The humming had turned into a louder 'mmm' sort of sound that was definitely human. His neck prickled with apprehension. Was it Kyle? Once at the top step, he nudged the door. It flew open and he shone the torch round the stone walls. The hayloft was lined with large hay bales. There was an overwhelming smell of last year's hay. As he rounded a stack of bales, his torch flickered over an object on the floor. He shone his torch over the shape to reveal a figure tied up and covered in an old, mouldy horse rug. His torch flickered over the face. It was Kyle, his eyes wide with fear and his mouth plastered with silver tape. But at least he was very much alive. Tristan moved to release him but then heard an almighty crash from somewhere behind him, then a searing pain in his skull as he felt himself falling.

Poppy laid in wait cursing herself. She should really had gone with Tristan. Anything would be better than this, just being sat in the cold, waiting. Her eyes peered into the darkness, straining as she followed Tristan's progress by his torch light. She heard an owl hooting and a dog or was it a fox barking in the distance. The darkness was now complete. She sat still every nerve tensed, as she watched and waited. The torchlight had now disappeared, so Tristan must be searching inside the barn, she reasoned. Supposing Kyle wasn't there, supposing they had got the whole thing completely wrong? She was so determined to believe the best in Kyle that maybe she was blind to the fact that he may have just gone off, disillusioned with his work. He may have been tempted into an easier lifestyle, fallen into bad company, got involved in drugs, anything really. Perhaps, she was just being horribly naïve?

The minutes turned into half an hour and still there was no sign of Tristan. Poppy stamped her feet and peered into the darkness. Suddenly, she was aware of a large orb of light approaching. Thank God! The light wobbled rhythmically as the person carrying it walked. Alarm crept down her spine. Something was very wrong. The light looked larger and brighter than Tristan's torch, she was sure of it. She scrambled around for her LED light and flashed once and waited. There was no corresponding response, nothing. She flashed again, her hands fumbling for her car keys. In a split second she made her decision and started up the engine, backing up and turning around. As she did so her headlights illuminated the face of the tall figure now running towards her. *Him? No, it couldn't be?* Poppy jammed her foot onto the accelerator, and raced back down the track, her heart hammering painfully in her chest.

# Chapter 28

Jamie listened patiently after an initial lecture about how foolhardy they had been.

'So, you and this Tristan Davies decided to take matters into your own hands and set about tracking Kyle using an app on his mobile?'

How did he manage to make her actions sound incredibly foolish and ill thought through? He was an expert at it, she realised.

'Yes, that's about the size of it. We were only going to have a quick look. But Tristan didn't come back. We had this signal to flash once for OK and twice for get the hell out of there. This guy came towards me and I flashed once, and he didn't flash back so I just came back...' She knew she was gabbling and incoherent.

'Right.' She could hear Jamie trying to be patient and understanding. 'Where were you exactly?'

'The app sent us out to past Market Leighton on to the A123 just past Jilthorpe. There is a tiny track off there and a stone barn about a mile or so up on the left.'

'OK. Now listen, this person that you saw, did you get a good look at their face? Think carefully.'

Poppy had hardly acknowledged it to herself. It just didn't make any sense. Yet, the tall, rangy figure with the smooth good looks, was unmistakable.

'Yes, it was Basil Lindley. He owns a racehorse, In The Pink and lives at Walton Hall.' And has lots of parties, she wanted to add, but thought she might sound completely mad or hysterical.

'Are you sure?'

'Yes, yes. I'm sure.'

'Why on earth would he kidnap Kyle Devlin? Any ideas?'

Poppy's head was swimming. 'No. I haven't the foggiest.' Foggy would certainly best describe her thought processes at the moment, she realised.

'Right. Take down my work mobile and I'll send some guys out now. Have you got a pen?'

Poppy fished in her bag for her diary and a biro and she took down the number. Her shaky handwriting betrayed her nerves.

'Now, this is very important. Where are you now and were you followed?'

Alarm pulsed through her. 'I'm at Kyle's and no, no I don't think so.'

'Right. I would feel much happier if you stayed at your grandparents tonight or went back home. I don't want you alone just in case you were followed. And Basil Lindley will certainly know where Tristan Davies lives.'

Poppy shuddered. Shit. She hadn't thought of that.

'Are you listening? Please go to your grandparents for the night and I'll catch up with you tomorrow. Alright?'

'OK, I will.'

'Poppy, will you promise me?'

'Yes, yes.'

'Take care, Poppy. I'll speak to you tomorrow, but if you have any problems or worries, anything at all then ring me.'

She thanked him, rang off and scooped up the piece of paper that had fluttered to the floor from her diary. It was in her grandmother's handwriting and was a copy of the horses listed in Basil's tip for the Yankee. She had absently stuffed the paper in her diary and had forgotten all about it. She read the horses names. In the Pink, Santa Lucia, Arctic Lion and Stellina Mia. She had heard of the first two, but the others rang a bell. Realisation flooded through her. Weren't they the horses that Tristan had said used to belong to the Manfredis? The two he'd spoken to Jim Day about? Was that why Tristan was

186

badly beaten up? He was asking too many questions about them and someone wanted him warned off? The Manfredis and Basil must be involved in some sort of betting coup but quite how it fitted with the complicated Yankee her grandmother had described, she had no idea.

She scooped up Tristan's laptop which might be useful, as even her grandparents had wifi. Tristan had helpfully left a post-it note attached to his screen with some writing on which Poppy assumed were passwords. As she was about to leave, she noticed Tristan's answer machine light blinking. He had two messages. She played them both. One was from a Graham Kent and the other from Matt his Private Investigator mate. Matt's message said it was urgent and that he had emailed some information to Tristan. She deleted the messages so that anyone breaking in wouldn't have access to them. As she drove, she tried to think. There must be some sort of betting scam going on, which explained the Manfredis and Basil being insistent that their horses all ran on tomorrow at Towcester, but how did any of this link to Kyle's disappearance. After all, Kyle was abducted when he had been simply wanting to confront the men who were implicated in the disappearance of young, vulnerable girls, one of whom had been his girlfriend. Somewhere, there must be link but for the life of her she just couldn't see it.

Tristan's head was pounding as he gingerly opened his eyes. His mouth tasted of blood. He was lying, bound with tape over his mouth with some sort of rough smelly rug laid over him. In the dim light he could make out Kyle similarly trussed up staring at him. Tristan tried to communicate with him, but it was difficult even to look at each other in the dark. He moved his arms and legs trying to work out how tightly the knots were tied. There. There was just a bit of give in the rope round his hands and his fingers could just reach the edge of the knot. He picked at it patiently, took a breather then tried again. He was almost sure there was even more give now and the knot felt looser, he was sure of it. He just had to keep at it and not drift off. He made himself pick at the rope for the count of twenty then rest for twenty. The effort was surprisingly tiring, especially when he felt so groggy. Again, he counted to twenty and then rested. The rope tore at his fingers as he pulled it. So, he decided to change the rhythm to tens. Pull at the knot for the count of ten then rest for ten. Come on, come on, he told himself. You can damned well do this.

When he rested, his eyes fell upon the outline of Kyle sat opposite him and he could feel Kyle's eyes upon him, willing him on. He just hoped that Poppy was safe and had had the good sense to drive away. He wondered if his assailant had gone after her. In which case, he told himself, he would have been preoccupied with chasing her and probably would have made a poor job of tightening the knots. Come on, come on he told himself. Somewhere he heard an owl hooting and the flapping of another bird. He kept up the rhythm patiently counting, pulling at the knot and then resting. He wondered what time it was and puzzled over what had happened, but he didn't reach any useful conclusions. The smell of the horse's sweat from the rug was strangely reassuring in its familiarity and he was grateful for the warmth the rug gave him.

Time past and he felt his resolve weakening. Surely, Poppy would have told the police and they would come? But suppose the assailant came back and moved them somewhere else? What then? It was a question of pride. He should have been more careful in looking for whoever it was that had bashed him over the head. It stood to reason that Kyle would have a guard and the gang, whoever was in it, would certainly send someone out soon. Then, it would be a different story. They had to get out now, otherwise anything might happen. And he knew he could do it, if he didn't give up. He thought about all the good things in his life, his family, racing career, the thrill of being sat on an amazing horse, as on as they soared over hurdle and ditches. The winner's enclosure and the cheers of the crowd. Poppy. Her relentless belief in what she did, her faith in Kyle and her determination to help him realise his potential. Then he thought about Melvin Clough and how everything had gone wrong since he had come on the scene. What he wouldn't give to be able to wipe that smirk off his face.

The adrenalin coursed through him at the thought of Clough's sly face. He wouldn't, couldn't let that bastard get away with what he had done. He pushed himself again. 1,2,3,4 by the count of 5, he felt the knot loosen and wriggled one hand free then another. Elation flooded through him and he ripped the tape off his mouth and then began to free his ankles.

'Don't worry there Kyle. We'll soon have you out of here, OK?' Kyle nodded and grunted. Tristan felt around for his torch which he reasoned he would have dropped in the attack. Surely, his attacker wouldn't have thought to pick it up. He scrambled around in the hay bales and felt something metallic and round. He switched on the light and shone the beam over Kyle. He looked dirty, dishevelled and smelt appalling but he appeared relatively unharmed. He began the task of untying his ropes and eventually helped him to his feet.

Kyle beamed.

'Thank the Lord. Do you have a drink? I'm parched.'

Tristan fished in his inside pocket for a small hipflask.

'Whiskey, do you?'

Then his attention was drawn by hovering lights and the distant sound of cars.

'Shit, supposing they've come back?' He turned off his torch light and peered through the open window. There were at least two vehicles, he realised. He beckoned to Kyle who walked towards him unsteadily.

'Do you feel able to make a run for it? We could make it to the woods over there and then back down onto the main road and back into Jilthorpe.' He felt for his 'phone in his pocket. Then he could ring Poppy when they were out of danger.

Kyle nodded. Then they heard car doors being opened as the headlights lit up the inky sky. They were back and this time they had reinforcements.

Tristan looked at Kyle and pointed to the hay bales. They stacked them so there was another higher row that they could hide behind. He motioned to Kyle to get down. They had to think of a plan urgently.

# Chapter 29

Millicent sat there in her pyjamas with George patiently listening whilst they sipped their cocoa. Poppy explained everything that happened including the missing girls and the betting scam. They occasionally looked at each, but otherwise sat in silence.

'Tristan was convinced there was something going on when Bennie was nobbled so to speak and then he was badly beaten up when he started asking questions.' Poppy fished in her diary for the slip of paper her grandmother had given her and spread it out on the table. 'I just can't figure out how the Yankee can be used in a betting scam. I suppose they could put enormous sums of money on each element of the bet, but wouldn't that alert somebody, the bookies, the racing authorities and so on?'

Millicent pursed her lips, thinking carefully.

'So, Basil Lindley is involved, is he?'

'Well, he gave you the tips and I saw him at the barn, so yes he seems to be the mastermind behind everything. And the Manfredis are in it up to their necks too.'

'Who are they?'

'Some other rich Italian owners.'

'But you did telephone the police about Kyle and Tristan, didn't you?'

'Yes, yes. I gave them the exact location. They should be there by now.'

George stood up and paced about. 'I think this calls for Betsy, don't you dear?'

Millicent nodded grimly. 'Yes dear. Basil might have followed Poppy.' With that George and Bertie left the room.

'Who's Betsy?'

'Oh, nothing to worry yourself about, dear. Now let's think about this betting scam.'

Poppy nodded and fished out Tristan's silver laptop.

'His Private Investigator mate left him a message saying he had emailed him some information.'

Millicent came and sat next to Poppy as they waited for the laptop to boot up. Thankfully the passwords were correct, though Poppy thought she really must speak to Tristan about his internet security or lack of it.

'I never really liked Basil Lindley, you know. His wife was a lovely woman and hinted at his gambling and womanising tendencies.' Millicent shuddered. 'Anyway, he was just too suave, too smooth.'

Poppy nodded. 'So, do you think he'll come here?'

Millicent nodded. 'Well, I'd would say it was highly probable, wouldn't you? But he doesn't scare me. George will protect us. Now let's have a look at those articles, shall we?'

Poppy was amazed at her grandmother's calm acceptance of the situation. Who would have thought it? She had always trusted her implicitly and if she wasn't worried, then why should she be.

'I'll just text my policeman contact, just in case.' Millicent just smiled enigmatically.

Having sent Jamie a quick message, Poppy tapped away on the keyboard and waited for the first article to open. When it did the contents made her gasp. It was a police report about Mafia activities in the UK being led by various families, the most notorious of which was the Castellano family. Paulo Castellano and his two sons were wanted in Italy for hideous crimes such as racketeering, prostitution, drug smuggling, blackmail and several murders. Paulo was named as the ringleader, closely followed by his two sons, Brando and Nico. The article had mug shots of all three. Poppy hadn't met Luca but clearly recognised the sons as the two men who had been at the yard with the two jockeys. It was crystal clear. The Manfredis were the Castellanos and were dangerous criminals, wanted in Italy and believed to be setting up other nefarious activities in Europe. In fact, she could tell them they were right here in the England in York and Walton of all places. So that was what was behind the grooming of young girls. It was an attempt to lure them into prostitution. She remembered Brando and his heart stopping good looks. How easy would it be for him to turn his attention to any girl, lead them on with stories of modelling careers, make up a modelling agency, provide drugs and develop a dependency then make them do unspeakable things. God, she even felt a moment's guilt at her own reaction to Brando. Damn. He was obviously the B that Sadie was referring to!

'That's the Manfredis! They are the Castellanos, a well-known Mafia family according to this. Shit!'

Millicent frowned at the swear word and grabbed the laptop off Poppy.

'Hmm. So that's it! I bet Lindley is in hock to the Mafia and has had to come up with a way of recouping his money. Audrey told me she had no idea how he managed to hang on to house after the divorce especially when he lost his business. Now, that would explain it.'

Poppy clicked on the second attachment. It was a confidential letter from the racing authorities asking the police to investigate several jockeys and racehorse trainers including Joey Gordan, Melvin Clough and Marcus Eden. It alleged that there were several betting anomalies lately and cited these people as being involved.

Millicent and Poppy peered at the screen, trying to take everything in.

'I still don't get how the betting scam works.' Poppy felt her brain was scrambled.

'I think we're about to find out...' Poppy followed Millicent's gaze. Silently and casually, Basil walked into the front room and sat down on the sofa opposite. He moved with the grace of a dancer. He was holding a pistol, aiming it directly at Poppy's head.

'Dear ladies. It's such a pity it's come to this, it really is.' Basil shook his head and looked at them with real regret. 'If only you and your jockey friend hadn't gone on asking questions. But you just wouldn't let it go, would you?'

Poppy gaped at the gun and sat stock still.

'Basil, we were just talking about you. Perhaps, you can help us out? We were just wondering how on earth your betting scam works? After all, you're not going to get very far putting large sums on in that Yankee, are you? The bookies will certainly smell a rat. Come on humour me, how are you planning to do it?'

Poppy glanced at Millicent in amazement. She was as cool as you like, still sat there in her pyjamas and slippers. Basil smiled, although Poppy wished he'd just put his gun down.

'Well, I'll tell you before I tie you up. It is rather clever though I say it myself. Firstly, you pick four very lightly raced but talented horses that you know are likely to win. So little raced that no-one really knows anything about then. Rank outsiders, if you like. Then you plan the betting. You see you are right about large single bets, quite right. But what about if you have a whole host of people placing small bets all at the same time? And complex bets like Yankees? They are virtually undetectable until it's too late. We tried the system out using trebles and it worked brilliantly. So, this next one is much more ambitious. You see I have organised a hundred people to place five bets each within a period of an hour. It's taken some organising as I have had to plan the areas very carefully so that they can find five bookies within the time. We should make several million pounds, all told.'

Millicent nodded. 'Well, that should do it. Ingenious, Basil. Absolutely ingenious.'

Basil was still smiling, a self-satisfied, smug smile. 'Well, I knew as a fellow gambler, you would appreciate it. That's why I gave you the tip.'

Poppy gasped. What the hell was going on?

'Oh, you didn't know? Well, your grandmother is a talented tipster. Ever heard of the Milliman? Well, Milliman and Millicent are one and the same person. Why don't you tell her? You see we're not so different after all.'

Millicent inclined her head slightly. 'But there is one big distinction, Basil. All my bets are entirely legal.'

Poppy swallowed hard. Millicent a racing tipster? She was beginning to think she hardly knew her grandparents at all.

'But what I don't get is how you can really predict the results of national hunt races? The horses can fall at any time.'

Basil nodded. 'Quite right, Poppy. But that's where the jockeys come in. You have to have a jockey who is prepared to do anything to win. You see, that's why we couldn't use Tristan. He's far too upstanding.'

Poppy had a horrible thought. 'So, I presume Jeremy and Laura are in on it too?'

Basil shook his head.' No, one dodgy trainer in Joey Gordan is quite enough and Jeremy is also very honest, if not a bit gullible. But no-one would ever suspect him.' Basil looked at his watch and reached for his holdall. Poppy wondered when George and Betsy might put in an appearance or Jamie for that matter. She hoped that Betsy was a code name for some police friend or military personnel. She glanced at Millicent who was still looking completely calm and looking steadily at Basil. So, she did the same. Despite the fact that in her peripheral vision she saw lights flickering through the curtains. At last, she thought.

What happened next was so sudden she thought she had imagined it. Her grandfather crept in behind the sofa where Basil was sitting, putting his fingers to his lips.  Goodness knows what he was planning to do.  She must try to help him, but how?

'What will happen to us?' Millicent's gaze was almost challenging.

Basil smiled. 'Well, of course, I haven't forgotten George, even though you thought I had.' Basil shook his head at Millicent, as though she was a naughty child. 'Did you really think you were going to get away with it? So, I was planning on tying you up and then sorting him out.'  He bent over delving in his holdall, his other hand still training the gun at Poppy, but his attention was distracted.  Poppy hadn't liked the way he said he wanted to 'sort out' George. She must do something. Poppy glanced at her foot and the gun in Basil's hand mentally rehearsing what she had to do.  Within a split second she had leapt up and kicked the pistol out of Basil's hand.  As it fell to the floor, she flicked it under the sofa. In an instant, George had yanked Basil to the floor and pressed his own gun to Basil's head. The move was polished and highly professional.

'Stay there or I will shoot!' he shouted.  Basil stayed completely still.

Millicent clapped her hands. 'Well done, both of you!  You see, Poppy, Betsy is your grandfather's old service revolver. He was in the Parachute Regiment for a few years in his youth. That was before he went into the bank, of course.' Poppy hadn't known this and looked on in amazement at her rather exceptional grandparents. To think that she had been worried about confiding in them, just hours before?

Millicent looked out of the window. 'I think the cavalry have just arrived...'


The shimmering lights Poppy thought she had seen became much brighter accompanied by full blown sirens. The house was flooded with policemen led by Jamie, with Tristan and Kyle in tow.

'What on earth?' Jamie was equally stunned by the scene before him. Basil was laid on the floor with his arms twisted behind his back and with George holding a gun to his head. He was still wearing his pyjamas and slippers. Millicent was still sitting in a queenly fashion as if this was an everyday occurrence. Basil was led off, chuntering and struggling, handcuffed to two burly officers. Poppy hugged Tristan, Kyle and her grandparents. She was gabbling about what she had found out.

'The Manfredis are really the Castellano family and are wanted for mafia type activities, so they are the ones that have been luring the girls on the promise of a career in modelling. Basil masterminded the whole thing because he owed lots of money to the Manfredis, I mean the Castellanos.'

Tristan grinned and ruffled Kyle's hair. 'Kyle, here, had almost worked it out and has been telling me on the way here.'

Kyle looked sheepish. 'Yes. I followed Louella before and recognised Brando from the photoshoot when he came to the yard. Then I heard you mention the app and thought I'd try it, but they saw Tristan and though I ran, they managed to catch me.'

Poppy beamed at him. 'I'm so glad you're both OK. I'm so sorry to have left you both at the barn, but I realised that something wasn't right and rang the police. Is that how you got out?'

Tristan shook his head. 'We managed to escape and made our way down into Jilthorpe where we saw the police.' He glanced at Kyle. 'We overpowered them by throwing a well placed hay bale or two and made a run for it.'
Jamie appeared from nowhere having stopped barking orders and muttering into his radio.

'Don't worry, Poppy. Several police cars went up the barn and most of the gang are in custody.'

It was over. Poppy suddenly felt overcome with emotion and terrible fatigue. Jamie caught sight of her pale face and put a proprietary arm around her shoulders. Poppy was just too damned exhausted to object. Tristan looked on, his expression inscrutable.

'What about a cup of tea?' suggested Millicent.

# Epilogue

It was mid December and a cold winter's day. Cold but clear with the sun just threatening to come out, perfect for an afternoon's racing at Kempton Park. Tristan had already ridden in a couple of races. He had been placed in both, but this was his last ride of day and definitely his best chance. Tristan was riding In the Pink in the prestigious Bollinger Champion Hurdle race which was run over three miles. Tristan felt the thrill of anticipation as the starter gave his orders and Pinkie surged forward, full of it. Mindful of Jeremy's orders, he tried to keep him mid field, but Pinkie was straining at the bit. They flew over fence after fence, clipping one and narrowly avoiding a faller at another. The sodden ground sprayed mud all over him and the horses, making it hard to see. The noise from the galloping hooves was deafening. He hastily wiped his goggles, so he could see the field ahead and consider his strategy as he rode. They moved through the field, so there were just the two horses ahead. A grey, ridden by a garrulous Irish jockey called Niall Casey in purple colours and a bay with Charlie Durrant aboard in red hoops. Both were in with a shout, so he had to try to contain Pinkie until the last fence or so.

Tristan tracked the red colours of the bay horse, as it pressed ahead. Charlie was definitely going for it and his horse looked full of running, whilst the grey to his left was beginning to fade. Niall tried to revive him, but then abruptly slowed down, knowing they were a spent force. There were just the two of them, the bay and Pinkie as they reached the last fence. Pinkie could hear the distant roar from the stands and instinctively knew they were near the finish line. Tristan steadied him to get the stride for the last fence and Pinkie pinged it, landing just ahead of Charlie's mount who looked like he was tiring slightly.

Pinkie felt full of running and took little persuasion to lengthen his stride, as Tristan pushed him on, rocking his body and waving his whip so that Pinkie could see it in his peripheral vision. All nerves and muscles were straining as Tristan focused on getting to the post first. From the corner of his eye, he saw Charlie rallying the bay who was starting to come back at them gamely. The crowd were really roaring now as Tristan pushed Pinkie forward into the next gear. The winning post was just in sight. Come on, come on, come on! The bay horse was nudging closer and closer, but Tristan pressed his legs against Pinkie, hands and heels urging him forward. The winning post flashed by them in a blur. They had done it!

Elation flooded through him and he punched the air in delight and patted Pinkie's sweat soaked neck, his chestnut coat now the colour of ginger cake. The steam was rising from him. He could just make out Kyle and Jeremy rushing over to him, both their faces wreathed in smiles. He caught his breath.

Charlie Durrant rode up to him and clapped Tristan's back. 'Well done, there. I thought we had it at one point. Anyway mate, it's great to have you back. Even if it means we'll win less races.'

Tristan grinned. 'Well, I can't let you have things all your own way.'

Kyle's figure became larger and larger as he approached grinning from ear to ear and clipped the lead rope to Pinkie's bridle.

'Well done, Tris. You rode a blinder. And you, boy, were amazing.' Kyle clapped Pinkie on the neck and led him towards the winner's enclosure. At the sight of Kyle's face and his evident passion for the sport, Tristan wondered how he could have ever doubted him. Poppy had had far more faith and understood that for care kids who were often rank outsiders in life they required someone who believed in them and were really batting for them. He felt ashamed at his scepticism. Still, he had an idea how he could make it up to him.

It was crowded, and the noise of cheering and congratulations was deafening. It was the Bollinger Champion Hurdle race after all and a significant win for all of them, with several cases of Bollinger champagne thrown in as well. The TV presenter asked for an interview and thrusting a furry microphone on a stick into his face. It was Laura Cummings, a pleasant woman who was perspiring slightly from the effort of jogging, to keep up with Pinkie's fast walk.

'I'm just going to speak to the winning jockey, Tristan Davies. Tristan, well done! Brilliant to win on your first afternoon's racing since your return. How do you feel after your time off? Bet you've been twiddling your thumbs at home, waiting for your bones to heal, haven't you?'

Tristan gave a wry smile. 'Well, I wouldn't quite say that...'

Laura, Poppy, Millicent and George had been cheering from the stands. Poppy was hoarse from urging them on.

'Bloody marvellous for all of us. I don't know about you, but I could do with a drink. Will you all join me? My treat.'

Laura's face was flushed under her furry head band, but she looked happier than she had in a long time. Soon, they were ensconced in the bar where Laura ordered a couple of bottles of champagne.

'What a brilliant end to the day and God knows we all need it. I'm sure Jeremy and the boys will join us shortly.' The waiter uncorked the bottle and poured out four glasses.

'Well, let's have a toast to Poppy, Tristan and Kyle. We can easily do it again when they get here of course, for their crime fighting.' The all clinked glasses and muttered, 'to Poppy, Tristan and Kyle.'

Poppy felt a deep flush spread over her. 'Well, George and Millicent certainly played their part.'

Laura surveyed them. 'Really?'

Millicent looked rather blank. 'No, it was nothing really.'

George smiled. 'Just got old Betsy out to assist that's all.'

Laura nodded, none the wiser. 'But seriously, I can't believe that Basil was up to his eyeballs in debt to the mafia and would get involved in a betting scam involving our yard. He was always such a charmer. But the Manfredis or rather Castellanos, well they certainly had me fooled, too.' She shook her head and clutched at Poppy's hand. 'We have so much to thank you for. I mean if Madeleine had got involved with Brando then who knows what could have happened, not to mention our reputation being in tatters if we'd become embroiled in a betting scandal.'

Poppy nodded. Laura had already told her about coming across a business card for the Boss Modelling Agency in Madeleine's pockets when she was doing the washing, so now recognised the enormity of what could have happened.

'Well, we can all be fooled by charming people. Villains don't exactly come with tattoos on their heads. It could have happened to anyone.'

They all looked at each other gravely, acknowledging the truth of this.

'Just tell me how Basil planned the betting again, I couldn't quite get my head round it?' Laura asked.

'Well, it is complicated. He had about a hundred or so people putting on complex bets, Yankees where you bet on any four horses on one particular day to win. Basil carefully selected little raced horses who were working very well at home but who the betting public knew very little about. The so-called layers went from several betting shops within a two hour period betting fairly small amounts on the same horses. So, the areas had to be quite carefully selected so that they contained at least five bookies within a certain radius.' Poppy paused, looking at the sea of expectant faces.

Laura nodded blankly.

'It must have taken some organising. Hence the parties to instruct the layers and the spies with binoculars, I suppose,' added George.

'Well, large single bets would easily be spotted and blocked by the bookies, but many small multiple bets laid in a short time frame would have been virtually undetectable,' continued Millicent, showing her knowledge of the betting world.

'Gosh, it was an ingenious plan, wasn't it? I suppose Basil is a very clever man,' commented Laura.

'But not quite clever enough,' muttered George darkly. 'He would have got away with several million pounds, had his plan come off.'

'So where are the police up to, do you know, Poppy, dear?' asked Millicent.

'The last I heard was that Basil was facing charges for fraud and kidnap. The Castellanos are all in prison and facing extradition to Italy but that may take a while as they are investigating all their crimes in the UK including the suspected murder of David and Tara Fenton. Melvin Clough is suspended pending investigations. So, it's all being sorted out, one way or another.'

Laura looked thoughtful. 'And what about the girls who were running away regularly?'

Poppy grinned. She was especially pleased about them. 'Well, they haven't gone missing again and are talking to the police about their experiences. They are receiving counselling, and all are much more settled and doing very well considering. We can't be certain, but it seems we stopped things just in time. The police have seized lots of indecent images of other girls though, which will be used as evidence in their case against the Castellanos. So together with their other crimes, they will be locked away for a very, very long time.'

'Wonderful. What a great result. You do such a worthwhile and important job, Poppy. Don't let anyone ever tell you any different.' Laura smiled with real warmth.

'So, how did you manage to run Pinkie with Basil being locked up for fraud? Did you have to talk to the rest of the syndicate? I'm surprised they're not here?' Poppy asked. She definitely hadn't noticed anyone other than Jeremy, Tristan and Kyle in the parade ring.

Laura grinned. 'Oh, I forgot to tell you. You see, Basil was in the process of selling his share in Pinkie anyway. He had persuaded the syndicate to do the same. I think he was planning on settling his debt with the Castellanos when he won his money and moving abroad. So, Pinkie has another owner who is new to racing. He wants Jeremy to buy him several more horses and has given him a blank cheque. Brilliant news isn't it?'

'How much of a blank cheque?'

Laura even looked a little shamefaced. 'Enormous, actually. Amazing. Can you guess who he is?'

They looked at each other speechless. Poppy looked round the room expecting the new owner to pop up at any minute.

'Well. We'll have to avoid Saturday afternoon meetings in the future. That's why he's not here today. Any ideas?'

Laura was bouncing up and down with excitement and they waited expectantly for her to tell them.

'Only bloody Tyler Dalton! You know the Manchester City midfielder. Can you believe it?'

Poppy laughed. He was another of the Blooms' foster children. Once a Bloom, always in Bloom they had said. And it certainly seemed to be true.

'Can you believe what?' asked Jeremy who had slipped in quietly with Tristan and Kyle. Tristan was dressed in a grey suit. Poppy had never seen him so formally dressed and had to admit that he scrubbed up rather well. Kyle looked flushed with happiness and rather shy.

'Oh, well done. Here you are. Get yourselves a glass, you lot. We were just having a toast to Poppy, Tristan and Kyle who saved us and many others from a terrible fate.'

Jeremy nodded gravely. 'No seriously.' He surveyed Poppy and Tristan. 'Who knows where we would be if you hadn't followed your instincts. I do owe you all an apology. Especially you, Tristan. I just thought it was sour grapes when Melvin careered into you and ruined Bennie's chances. I can't apologise enough. And you have been a superstar, Poppy. From what I hear, Kyle and many other kids like him are lucky to have you on their side.'

Tristan met Poppy's eye and smiled, rather embarrassed at all the fuss. Kyle just beamed.

There was a silence as they all sipped their champagne.

'Anyway, I was just telling them all about Tyler Dalton buying Pinkie and giving you a blank cheque to buy some more quality horses.'

Jeremy flushed with delight. 'Yes. He had quite an interest in racing. He has been following the tipster Milliman for a while but now wants to get into racing itself. Splendid, isn't it? So, we have Milliman to thank too, whoever he is.'

Millicent glared at Poppy, but she wasn't about to say anything. She had already been sworn to secrecy. Her grandmother was not yet ready to reveal her new role. But she couldn't resist a little hint.

'Or she is...'

'Indeed.' Jeremy glanced at Kyle. 'Anyway, with all these new horses I have been thinking that Tristan might need some assistance, so how about that training you were asking about? I have been in touch with the Northern Racing College in Doncaster so perhaps you'd like to join us as a conditional jockey?'

Kyle looked stunned. 'Really? That's brilliant. I won't let you down, guv.' Kyle was pink with delight. He turned to Poppy. 'What do you think?'

'I think it's marvellous and very well deserved. Anyway, it won't be up to me. Tina is back from sick leave next week, so I won't be around too much from now on, I'm afraid.'

Kyle's face immediately fell. There was a collective sigh. Tristan's expression was hard to read.

Jeremy harrumphed. 'Well, we can't have that! Don't young people have rights these days and all that? If Kyle wants you as his social worker, then surely the powers that be can't ignore him? It's outrageous. I shall get onto your boss, Andrea wasn't it?'

Poppy smiled knowing exactly what the outcome of that conversation would be. Perhaps, she would still be driving out to Walton after all. She found the thought pleased her.

'I shall talk to her myself,' added Kyle flushing. 'Tina was OK but you've been brilliant.' Poppy beamed with pleasure. On some days you just had to count your blessings, and this was definitely one of those days.

Millicent glanced from Poppy to Tristan. 'So how are things going with that policeman chappie, Jamie, wasn't it?'

Poppy flushed. 'Well, they're not actually…' Honestly, if she didn't know any better, she would have thought her grandmother was conducting some covert matchmaking. But Millicent looked the picture of innocence. Poppy resisted the urge to kick her in the ankles. She glanced uncertainly at Tristan. He looked so handsome and eminently fanciable. She tried to cover her embarrassment at the thought.

'Lovely champagne, isn't it?'

Tristan grinned and looked at her meaningfully. 'Well, I've won a case of the stuff, so you'll have to help me drink it. It may take a while.'

Millicent gave her a huge wink. Poppy looked at Tristan and smiled.

'Well, you know what? I think I could develop quite a taste for it.'

'And whilst we're at it, I think we might just have another case for us to solve. Charlie Durrant has been telling me about a horse he rode a couple of times and the thing is he's convinced it *wasn't* the same horse. He's sure that the trainer was trying to pass it off as the same horse, but it was in a different league. A bit like going from a Nissan Micra to a Porsche. Or a Renault to an Audi…'

Poppy swatted his arm at the criticism of her car, but her eyes were gleaming as she scooped up her glass.

'Go on. Tell me all about it...'

# About Charlie De Luca

Charlie De Luca was brought up on a stud farm, where his father held a permit to train National Hunt horses, hence his lifelong passion for racing was borne. He reckons he visited most of the racecourses in England by the time he was ten. He has always loved horses but grew too tall to be a jockey. Charlie lives in rural Lincolnshire with his family and a variety of animals, including some ex-racehorses.

Charlie has written several racing thrillers which include: Hoodwinked, The Gift Horse, Twelve in the Sixth and Making Allowances.

You can connect with Charlie via twitter; @charliedeluca8 or visit his website. Charlie is more than happy to connect with readers, so please feel free to contact him directly using the CONTACT button on the website.

www.charliedeluca.co.uk

If you enjoyed this book, then please leave a review. It only needs to be a line or two, but it makes such a difference to authors.

Praise for Charlie De Luca.

'He is fast becoming my favourite author.'

'Enjoyable books which are really well plotted and keep you guessing.'

'Satisfying reads, great plots.'

Printed by Amazon Italia Logistica S.r.l.
Torrazza Piemonte (TO), Italy

16844934R00121